Montana Rescue

Billy Hall

DEO VOLENTE
PUBLISHING

Billy Hall, *Montana Rescue*
© 2010 by Bill D. Hallsted
Published by Deo Volente Publishing
P.O. Box 119
Humboldt, TN 38343

Printed in the United States of America

Cover photograph by John Taylor.

ISBN 10: 0-9753446-4-1
ISBN 13: 978-09753446-4-4

Chapter

One

She had to get his guns to him! She had to put the baby down. She had to get him a pistol. No! She had to get both pistols. She would hand him one, and keep the other. That wouldn't be enough! There were too many of them.

Myra Hackett stifled a frightened sob. She ran for the rocking cradle Tom had made so lovingly. She laid baby Deborah in it as gently as she could, given her haste. She wheeled to the mantel and grabbed the pair of heavy Colts.

Forcing herself to take a deep breath, she checked the loads in each. She nodded absently as she closed the cylinders. As an after-thought, she cocked the hammer on both weapons. It took too long! She had to lay one down to use both thumbs to pull back one of the hammers until it clicked into place. Then she had to lay it down and do the same with the other. She hurried to the door. Taking another ragged breath, she opened it and stepped outside.

She held her hands behind her back, keeping the pistols out of sight behind the full skirt of her dress. She willed herself to breathe normally.

"Walk slowly," she told herself sternly. "Smile a little. Sunday stroll. I'm just joining my husband to greet our company."

Her breath kept catching in her throat. Her heart pounded so hard she knew the Indians could hear it, clear across the yard. They were watching her. She willed her feet to slow down, but she knew they were walking with a will of their own.

She gained her husband's side and stood against him. His arm went instinctively around her waist. She could feel him stiffen slightly as his hand brushed one of the hidden weapons. She felt the heavy breath of relief and satisfaction as he took one of the guns from her grip.

"You have fine woman," the Indian facing Tom said. "Flaming hair is good medicine. You give cows now."

"I've been trying to tell you," Tom said, squaring his shoulders and speaking with a new ring of confidence, "I'm not one of those big ranchers. I've only got a few cows. I can't afford to give you any. My wife's father always gives several cows every year for the use of the land. If you want more, you'll have to talk to him."

"You give!" the Indian replied flatly. "You give, or we take. If we take, we take all. Maybe we take woman with flaming hair, too."

Tom stepped away from his wife. He brought his hand around so the Colt was visible to the line of roughly a dozen Indians ranged before him.

"You ain't takin' nothin'!" he said hotly, his chin jutting forward. "Now, I want to be friends with you and with your people, but I can't have you takin' my stuff and threatenin' my wife. Now you best all ride out."

There were several audible grunts when the pistol appeared. The Indians' attitude changed perceptibly. The speaker stared silently and impassively at Tom, as though measuring his mettle.

Myra took advantage of the lull to take a step backward and bring her own hand into view, holding the other heavy pistol. A murmur of surprise and, she thought, of appreciation, rippled through the Indians.

The spokesman for the Indians nodded. "Flaming hair is good medicine," he repeated. "A warrior with such a woman should have much honor."

"She is a fine woman," Tom agreed. "Now, I'll have to ask you again to all ride out. I got nothin' more to say."

The Indian studied him for a long moment, then turned to the line of warriors. He spoke in their own tongue. Several nodded. Some lifted the reins of their ponies as though to ride away. The speaker turned back to Tom.

"It is good to have strong men with good women in this country. You go back to your house now. We will leave."

Tom hesitated. He was reluctant to turn his back on that many Indians. He was just as reluctant to appear belligerent and spoiling for a fight. He didn't understand Indian customs at all. If he backed away, facing them as he returned to the house, would it antagonize them? If he turned his back to them, wouldn't that show trust and acceptance? If he refused to do either, wouldn't that almost force them to fight?

He nodded to Myra. "Then we will part as friends," he said to the Indian.

Deliberately he turned his back to the line of warriors. Myra stepped beside him, and they began to walk toward the open door of their house.

A tingling sensation flew up and down Myra's back. She could feel their eyes. She could feel their eyes on the back of her skirt. She tried to walk without swinging her hips. The door was so far away! There was no sound, except the occasional stomp of a horse's hoof.

They were half way to the door when Tom grunted. Myra whirled her head to look, but Tom was already lying on the ground. An arrow protruded from the back of his neck.

She spun around as four of the Indians broke from the line and raced their horses toward her, yelling wildly. She stifled a scream and raised the still cocked pistol toward them. It roared and one of the Indians toppled from his horse. She gripped the gun with both hands, using both thumbs to pry the hammer back to a cocked position.

The hammer clicked its readiness and she raised the gun again. A sharp pain paralyzed her arm. The gun roared harmlessly into the air.

She grabbed her arm and looked desperately toward her fallen husband. Only then did she see three arrows besides the one in his neck. He lay without moving, clearly dead.

Three Indians had hold of her. Their smell was strange and overpowering. Their hands were coarse and rough as they grabbed her and began exploring her body eagerly. She felt herself thrown violently to the ground, with one of the Indians on top of her, pawing at her skirt.

A barked word she did not understand penetrated her panic. The hands ceased their probing and withdrew as though the feel of her skin had burned them. The one on top of her leaped to his feet and stood aside. She struggled to her feet, looking wildly about for the gun that had been knocked from her grip.

She spotted it lying in the dirt. She started to move toward it, but her way was instantly blocked. She looked into the expressionless eyes of the Indian who had spoken to Tom. He spoke English! She could reason with him!

"What have you done to my husband?" she sobbed almost hysterically. "How could you do that? He trusted you! Let me go! Get off our land! What is the matter with you?"

Her torrent of words was stopped by a stunning blow from the back of the Indian's hand. Her head reeled as her hand flew to the spot on her cheek, suddenly aflame with pain.

"Red hair will make good medicine for Many Thunders," the Indian said. He looked around slowly at the others. "This one is mine. I will take her."

She tried to answer, but her heart was in her throat. She could not speak. She looked again at her husband. He lay without moving.

Four Indians came out of the door of their rough cabin. One wore Tom's good hat her father had given him at the wedding two years ago. All carried blankets, trinkets, and what jewelry she owned. One held her baby! Deborah! The Indian carried her negligently, by one foot. She was crying frantically, pawing at the air with tiny hands. He grinned and held her aloft, saying something in the strange tongue she could not understand.

She forgot the stinging of her cheek and the ringing in her head. She screamed, "My baby!"

She ran to the Indian, grabbing desperately for her child. Deborah saw her and reached her tiny arms imploringly toward her mother.

The Indian laughed and lifted the infant higher, keeping her just out of reach of Myra's flailing arms. The three danced a sadistic step of reach and turn, with the Indian turning always away from her, keeping the baby just out of her reach.

A barked command stopped the game. It was the same Indian again. Many Thunders. That's what he said his name was. The warrior with her child looked hesitant, then allowed her to grab the screaming infant and clutch it to herself.

Two Indians rode from the corral with the only two horses she and Tom owned. They whooped and yelled as they led the horses at a run, stopping in a cloud of dust.

He was standing in front of her again. She clutched Deborah to herself more tightly, as though to shield herself from this strange, brutal creature. His hands ran through her hair, over her shoulders. He felt her upper arms, assessing her strength. He felt her breasts, her stomach. She held herself sternly still, refusing to react to the violation of her person.

He spoke, addressing her directly for the first time. "Many Thunders will take woman with hair like fire. You will ride with us. You will not run away. You will do as Many Thunders says. You will please me. If you do not, your child will be thrown to the coyotes. If you still do not, you will no longer be mine. Then the others will all share you. Get on horse."

There were no saddles. The Indians rode on blankets thrown across their horses. Some were held in place by rawhide thongs. Her horse and Tom's had nothing. The Indians were all mounted. She knew she had no choice. She could ride with them, or Deborah would die. So would she, but more slowly. Much more slowly.

Stifling a panicked sob, she held Deborah on top of her horse's withers, gripping the horse's mane and the baby with the same hand that held the reins. Then she grasped the mane with her other hand and lunged with all her might to mount the nervous animal.

She was not the typical Wyoming homesteader's wife. She had not ridden a horse bareback since she was a girl. On her parents' farm in Missouri she used to ride the plow horses whenever she could. They were great horses. When she was seated on their high, broad backs she felt like a queen surveying her kingdom, and she rode them every chance she got. It was only that experience that enabled her to get on the horse with no stirrup to assist her.

When her father had sold the farm and moved them to Wyoming Territory, the work horses were only used for putting up hay. She had not ridden bareback since.

As she settled on the horse's back she clutched Deborah to her again. She was still screaming in terror, and Myra tried to talk to her to soothe her fears. Knowing nothing else would soothe the child, she unbuttoned her blouse and began to nurse her. She thought Many Thunders almost nodded approval as he wheeled his horse and led the party from the yard.

Myra thought suddenly of the Indian she had shot. She whirled her head to scan the yard, but there was no Indian lying there. Three of the warriors bore recent wounds, so she finally decided he must be among them.

"I didn't even kill the only one I managed to shoot," she scolded herself.

They rode swiftly northward across the high rolling plains. They rode mostly along the bottoms of draws and along creeks, never along the ridges. Whenever they had to cross an area of visibility, two warriors rode ahead. Dismounting, they crawled to the top of the hill and scanned the country carefully. Only when they signaled an all-clear would the rest of the party advance.

They had ridden nearly three hours when Many Thunders stopped the party. He spoke in their own language. All but two warriors rode away over the hill. The two who remained with them were both wounded. She sat her horse nervously, waiting to be told what to do. She was told nothing.

Deborah began to fuss. One of the Indians gestured toward her and barked something Myra could not understand. She reasoned they wanted the baby to be silent.

Hurriedly she undid the front of her blouse again, knowing the only way to silence the baby was to nurse her again. She waited for the Indians to politely turn away. They only watched with obvious and open interest.

Deborah fussed again, gaining insistence and volume. Why wouldn't they at least look away? The Indian barked that word again, gesturing emphatically at the baby. They would kill her if she didn't silence her! But she couldn't just go ahead and nurse her with them so openly watching! She had to nurse her! What was the matter with these people?

Choking back her embarrassment and anger she opened the front of her blouse and held the baby to her breast. She took it eagerly, and Myra remembered that except for the very brief time as they had left the yard she hadn't fed the child for a long while. The two Indians watched without expression. They never looked away. They never looked at each other. They said nothing. They just watched.

Several shots sounded from across the hill, followed at once by a chorus of yells. More shots rang out, then a woman's scream floated on the breeze.

Almost an hour later the party returned over the hill. One Indian was obviously dead, tied across his horse. Another gripped the reins of a horse that held another young woman. The group galloped back to the three who were waiting, showing off several scalps and an odd collection of captured booty.

The woman was hysterical. Her voice was high pitched and out of control. She was screaming something and crying and yelling things Myra could not understand.

"Stop screaming, or they will do terrible things to you," Myra told her urgently. "Stop screaming!"

The woman would not, or could not. One of the Indians dismounted and walked to her. He looked toward Many Thunders. The leader nodded. The Indians jerked the woman from her horse. Throwing her to the ground, he stuffed a rag into her mouth. Others of the group joined him. Pieces of the woman's clothing began to appear from within the circle of warriors. They began to laugh, and to shout things to each other in their own tongue.

Myra turned away, unable to think. What should she do? What could she do? She tried to shut her ears against the horrible sounds coming from the group. She still heard every sound. Even with the rag stuffed into her mouth, the woman continued to sob. Myra willed herself not to listen. The Indians shouted encouragement and challenges to one another. Myra still heard every sound the woman made.

She looked wildly about. Only Many Thunders and the two most severely wounded remained on their horses. He was not watching the scene on the ground. He was watching her.

She was startled by the expression in his eyes. He looked like he approved what she was doing. But she was doing nothing! Nothing! What could she could do? She looked into the eyes of Many Thunders. In that instant she knew with certainty why he was not joining the others in their sordid revelry. He was saving all his energy for her!

She jerked her eyes away. She studied her baby, avoiding looking into the Indian's eyes again. As she looked into the contented face of her baby, she knew she would do whatever it took to save the child's life, and her own so that she could care for her.

She didn't know how long she sat there. It seemed a long, long time. At long last Many Thunders barked an order. Reluctantly the group broke off their depraved recreation and mounted their horses. The woman lay quivering and sobbing, naked to the merciless sun. She made no effort to cover herself, or to remove the dirty rag from her mouth. She just lay there, naked, bleeding, horribly bruised, twitching spasmodically.

Whooping and hollering, the group rode off at a gallop. One of them slapped Myra's gray gelding on the rump. He leaped to a gallop to keep up. She clutched her baby to her breast and concentrated desperately on staying atop the lunging horse.

§§§

Thirty miles to the south, Levi Hill abruptly stopped what he was doing. The lariat hung limp in his hand. The bronc he was getting ready to rope stood nervously against the far side of the corral.

Levi looked around uneasily. Something had passed through his mind. He knew what it was. He had no idea where it came from, or why. It felt like a cold wind. It blew downward across the back of his neck. It blew an empty queasiness into his stomach. He was suddenly and inexplicably afraid. His hand brushed reassuringly at the Colt .45 tied low on his hip.

An old scene replayed itself in his mind. Huddled in a clump of sage brush, he sobbed silently as Indians pillaged the shattered wagon train. His parents and his brother lay among the dead. That same cold wind was on him then. It was that cold wind that had caused him to crouch in the brush minutes before the Indians had attacked. It had saved his life. From that moment he had known himself fated for something different than other men. He simply had no idea what that fate was to be.

The memory wakened the pain that was never far below the surface of his mind. With it, that sense of imminent danger sharpened his senses.

His eyes darted around. Nothing seemed out of place. The activity in the S R Bar ranch yard continued routinely. He could see or hear nothing amiss. Still, the feeling was there. Something was wrong. Something was happening that smelled of great danger and death. It was remote, but he was, somehow, tied to it. It was his fate, his destiny. He just didn't know what it was.

Shrugging his broad shoulders, he advanced toward the nervous horse.

Chapter

Two

"The war's been over a long while," he drawled softly. The saloon fell deathly quiet.

The answer came just as softly. The words hardly made the long black moustache move. "If the war's over, how come you're still wearin' that Johnny Reb shirt?"

Jim Keller knew how much depended on his answer. The shirts were all he had kept from the war, now four years behind him. "Seems a shame to throw away a perfectly good shirt," he said, trying to keep any edge from his voice.

"Seems more to me like lookin' for trouble," the dark cowboy responded. "Wyoming Territory ain't exactly Johnny Reb country."

Jim glanced around at the saloon's attentive customers. All activity had stopped. Everybody seemed to be holding their collective breath, awaiting his answer. "I ain't askin' for no trouble," he said. "What is it you want?"

"I want you to give me that shirt," his antagonist replied. "We're gonna have us a little ceremony here, and burn the stinkin' thing."

Jim looked the man over carefully. The .44 on his hip showed a great deal of wear. The butt was polished by repeated and consistent contact with the palm of the man's hand. The holster was tied down. The strap over the hammer, that held the gun in place when its use was not expected, was unfastened and tucked behind the holster where it would not interfere with a quick draw. It was evident the small man was a gunman in search of a victim. Keller pushed his large frame away from the bar. He let his own hand drift to inches away from his own gun. "I reckon not," he said, still not raising his voice. "If you want the shirt off my back, I reckon you'll have to take it off. And I reckon you're too much of a yellow-bellied sow-suckin' polecat to do that."

The smaller man's eyes flashed. There was a sudden scramble of people moving out of the expected line of fire from the two men. They now faced each other, two feet away from the bar.

"Then I'll just have to take it off your dead body." The excited flush had left the smaller man's face, leaving it strikingly more pale than his dark complexion had seemed. The change of color made the stubble of beard seem even blacker than before. The covering of blackheads that crossed his nose made it look as though a stubble of beard grew there as well.

Keller sighed, "Why, you scrawny little son-of-a-buck, if you think you can, I reckon you'd just as well have at it."

There was a barest instant of hesitation. The smaller man's hand streaked for his gun. It was just clearing the holster when the .44 in Jim's hand roared. A cloud of gunsmoke slightly obscured the startled expression that crossed the man's face. He looked at Jim's gun as though trying to understand where it had come from. His eyes moved up to meet the tall stranger's, but they weren't focusing right any more.

The gun slipped from his fingers and thudded softly on the sawdust that covered the floor. He collapsed forward and lay without moving.

Voices exploded suddenly, erupting from all corners of the saloon. Jim holstered his gun as a soft voice spoke at his elbow. "Best duck out the back way," it said. "I'll show you. You ain't got much chance o' bein' treated fair, even if nobody liked Murdock anyway."

Jim looked into the brown wrinkled face of an old cowboy and nodded. They slipped wordlessly along the bar, down a narrow hall, and out the back door.

"Wait here an' I'll get your horse," the old man said. "Which one is he?"

"The big bay gelding. JK on the left shoulder," Jim replied. The wiry oldster re-entered the back door of the bar. In minutes that seemed to Jim like hours, he rode into sight several buildings down the alley, riding Jim's horse.

As he approached and slid down, Jim took his place in the saddle. "Ride down the alley, then swing east to that draw. You can follow it and keep out of sight till you're a mile outa town," he advised. "Good luck."

"Thanks," Jim replied, nudging his horse to a trot.

As he followed the old cowhand's suggestion, he found himself able to leave town totally unseen. He rode quickly but quietly, grateful to escape any further trouble. He was several miles beyond the edge of town when he began to relax.

"Well, Tug," he told his horse, "the hate them sow-suckers carry just seems to stay on and on, don't it? Some o' them road apples just won't never let it die."

The horse offered no answer, except to twitch his ears as he walked briskly among the scrubby sage brush of the Wyoming foothills. A cloud of gloom settled across Jim's mind. The war had been over more than four years. The hate remained. Would it ever fade?

Every hour he climbed to the top of a ridge and carefully scanned his back trail. "I doubt if them scroungy chicken stealers will set out to look fer me, but you never know," he told himself aloud, explaining his caution to himself. He saw no signs of pursuit.

That night he camped near a small spring. He waited until after dark, then built a small fire where its glow could not be seen from more than fifty yards away. As soon as he finished his supper he put it out again, and rolled into his blankets
.

The next morning he climbed a nearby ridge and scanned the country in all directions for a long while. Satisfied, he returned to his camp site, built a fire, and made his breakfast. When he had finished breakfast he heated some water over the fire and shaved carefully, using the large knife he carried on the side of his belt away from his gun. As he started to shave he scowled at the knife, then stropped it on his boot top until it was returned to an edge that pleased him. He shaved quickly and cleanly.

He rode out while the sun was still within a short arm's reach of the eastern horizon, shining directly behind him. His eyes constantly scanned the country around him, noting every detail of land and sky.

It was late morning when he sensed it. It was almost a toss-up, whether he or the horse first snapped to attention. He had no idea what he had heard or felt. The horse at least knew the direction. His head was up and his ears pointed toward the top of a nearby ridge.

He had been riding along the bottoms of the draws, as he wound his way toward the mountains, standing purple against the western sky. It wasn't that he was hiding, or running. It was just a long established pattern and he adhered to it without thought.

Now he drew up sharply and sat in his saddle, listening intently. He heard nothing.

Slipping his .44-40 carbine from its saddle scabbard, he slid silently to the ground. Following the direction his horse's ears pointed, he climbed the ridge.

As he neared the top, he removed his flat-crowned hat and laid it by a clump of sage brush. Crawling on all fours, he approached the crest of the ridge carefully. The last several feet he negotiated on his stomach, squirming silently through the sparse grass.

He selected a clump of brush that should command a view over the crest and crawled to it. Using it as a shield against searching eyes, he raised his head far enough to see.

He caught his breath and moved his rifle to a firing position, then waited, thinking fast. A dozen Indians sat their horses in a line in the yard of a homestead. A man and a woman stood talking to one of the Indians. Jim was more than five hundred yards from the nearest of them. It was way too far for a shot from a .44-40.

He began to look desperately for cover that would allow him to approach unseen, but could see none. From the other direction he could approach to within fifty yards of the house unseen, but from this direction he could move no closer than where he was.

"It'd take me an hour to go around," he muttered to himself silently.

As he watched, the man and woman turned their backs on the Indians and began to walk stiffly toward the house. "What are you doin', you stupid horse collar?" Jim exclaimed softly. "Don't do that! Turn around!"

He lifted his rifle to try an impossibly long shot at one of the Indians who was fitting an arrow to his bow, but he was already too late. Four arrows flew straight and true. The homesteader pitched forward to lie motionless on the ground.

The woman whirled and lifted the pistol she carried. Jim saw the Indian tumble from his horse before the sound of the gun reached him. He saw her try desperately to cock the hammer of the big Colt to fire again, but she had no time. The gun flew from her hand as an Indian swung his bow like a club. Several Indians grabbed the woman and threw her to the ground.

Jim lifted the rifle again, deciding to risk his own hair to distract them from their obvious intent with the woman. He saw the Indian's leader gesture and knew he was speaking, so he held his fire.

The Indians holding the woman down released her and she jumped to her feet. He could see her screaming at the Indian leader. He slapped her with the back of his hand.

Several Indians emerged from the house, carrying a baby by one foot, as well as other things they considered of value. The woman ran to the baby. The Indian holding it taunted her with it, holding it just out of her reach as she frantically tried to reach it.

Another word from the leader ended that game. The woman grasped her baby, and clung to it feverishly. Other Indians brought the horses from the corral. The Indian leader gestured at one of the horses, and the woman, still holding her baby, managed to climb aboard it. They rode out of the yard, riding swiftly.

Jim did not move until they were out of sight. When they were, he withdrew from the brow of the hill, then sat down on the ground. "Well, now, Jim Keller, you just got yourself into one real fine pickle," he said aloud.

He took his hat off again and scratched his head. "Now what are you goin' to do? You can ride on, and forget it. They'll probably take care o' the woman, okay." He nodded his head vigorously as though agreeing with himself. "Yeah, they'll take care of her. She'll end up bein' one o' the Indian's squaws. Prob'ly the leader's, what with that red hair o' hers. I reckon there's worse things."

He looked at the ground, then continued to himself. "Or, she might end up bein' raped by the whole bunch of 'em. They was obviously figgerin' to, when the one stopped 'em."

He stood up and began to pace the ground in a circle around his horse. He stopped and glanced up at the sun. "You could just mind your own business. Or, you could ride along an' try to pick 'em off, one or two at a time. O' course, if you did that, they'd come a-hellin' jist as soon's you got the first one."

He shook his head and took his hat off yet again. He scratched behind his right ear. "They's too many fer ya to take on alone, thet's all there is to it," he said, shaking his head emphatically.

He put his hat back on, pulling it down snugly. "Or, maybe you could just sorta tag along an' wait for a chance, and maybe figger out a way to get 'er away from 'em."

He sat down on a large rock, turning over the possibilities for several minutes. Finally he sighed and got to his feet. "I just can't ride away like I never saw it," he apologized to himself. "I'll prob'ly end up gettin' scalped like some tin-horn prairie dawg eater, but at least I gotta try."

He returned to his horse. Mounting, he began to follow the way the Indians had gone. A knot in his stomach testified to the feeling that he had made a decision that would cost him a great deal.

§ § §

Jim Keller wasn't the only one to sense the danger. Levi Hill had just finished topping off the bronc he was beginning to break. It had been a tough ride, but an exhilarating one. Now, as he walked toward the bunkhouse, he stopped dead in his tracks. It was there again. That icy wind blew through the chambers of his mind, leaving him shivering, cold and afraid. He looked around nervously. He could see nothing out of place.

He changed his course and walked to a small knoll behind the ranch yard. He looked long and hard in all directions, but could see nothing in any way alarming.

The feeling was still there, though. He knew that sense of danger like an old friend. Or an old enemy. He just had no

idea what was prompting its intrusion into his life at this
time. He very well knew every time that feeling returned
his life was turned upside down, and things were never the
same again.

Frowning, he headed back to the bunkhouse. Even though
the rancher and his wife had raised him, he felt more at
home with the hands, so he lived in the bunkhouse. It was
home. Even there, though, he couldn't keep his hand from
hanging close enough to brush the well-worn butt of his Colt
45.

"Hey, Levi."

He whirled. The .45 appeared in his hand as if had sprouted
from his fingers. A young cowboy stopped in his tracks,
turning pasty white
.

"Hey! Take it easy! It's me, Sandy."

Levi holstered the gun, a sheepish expression on his face.
"Sorry. I'm sorta jumpy today."

"How's come?"

"Danged if I know. I just got the funniest feeling I'm about
to get shot at or something. I feel like the hair on the back of
my neck's standing straight up in the air."

"Premonition," Sandy replied with conviction.

"Whatd'ya mean?"

"You sense somethin' comin'. My ma used to have 'em.
She had the second sight, she called it. She had some funny
feelin', she said, when somethin' awful was about to happen.

The day my pa got killed, Ma, she knowed it a'ready afore it actually happened. Just had that funny feelin', and started to bawlin'. She just didn't know what she was bawlin' about till they come an' told her."

"I never believed in that stuff," Levi responded.
At least he told himself he didn't. Nevertheless the feeling was there, and it wouldn't go away. Deep within himself he knew it was right. Something was happening, somewhere. He just had no idea what it was, or why it was going to completely alter the fabric of his life again.

Chapter Three

The night was long. So long it seemed at last she had grown old, and a long life had passed. Now she was just an old woman, carrying the husks of dead memories that had been her life. Was it just yesterday? No. It couldn't have been. It was when she was young. It was some other life. It was long ago and far away.

After the raid on the other ranch and the extended rape of the captive woman, her captors had grown excited about something. Myra thought one of them had seen something, looking back across the way they had come, but she could not understand. Two of the warriors had ridden away along their back trail.

The others had started up again. One of the wounded warriors fell from his horse. They stopped and examined him. He was dead. She had heard no word of complaint from him. She had no idea he was as sorely wounded as he was. She wondered momentarily if he were the one she had shot. Suddenly she hoped he was.

The Indians said nothing. They picked up their dead companion and lashed him across his horse. Then they rode on. Time ceased to have meaning, but they had ridden a long way. Somewhere, she no longer even knew what direction they were traveling, they stopped to water their horses. Many Thunders told her to get down from her horse.

When her feet struck the ground, she could not feel it. She could not stand. She fell against the Indian. He grabbed her, holding her roughly at arm's length until her legs regained enough feeling to allow her to stand.

"Make water," Many Thunders commanded. "We will not stop for yet a long time."

She needed to. She desperately needed to. The warriors did so, openly and with no hint of modesty, whenever they stopped. She could not. They would not watch her do that! But she had to. Yet she could not!

She handed her baby wordlessly to the Indian leader. He took a step backward, a look of shocked disbelief passing momentarily across his features. He said something in his own tongue, and pointed emphatically to the ground.

Myra stepped away from the horses and laid the baby carefully on the ground. She did as she was commanded, trying to keep herself as well covered with her skirt as she could. It was such a relief! She had had no opportunity to relieve herself since the Indians had attacked.

She knew Deborah must be just as uncomfortable. She hadn't been changed all day. Many Thunders barked an order, and the Indians remounted. She made a decision. "I have to change my baby," she said.

The Indians all stopped abruptly. They stared at her, then

looked, as one man, at Many Thunders. Myra ignored them.
She knelt beside her baby. Removing the incredibly soaked
and dirty diaper, she cast it aside. She wiped the baby as
clean and dry as she could with handfuls of grass. Then
she ripped a large piece from her petticoat, making a crude
diaper for the child. When she had fastened it in place, she
walked to her horse.

It took a supreme effort to get herself and the baby both onto
the back of the horse again. As she did, sharp pain stabbed
through her legs and buttocks. She bit her lip to keep from
making any sound. She would not give them the satisfaction
of hearing her cry out.

Wordlessly Many Thunders lifted his reins and rode off. The
rest fell in behind him.

Night descended. They did not stop. The grueling pace
continued without letup. About midnight, as nearly as she
could guess, they stopped again, briefly. She needed no
command this time. She knew that whatever she needed to
do, she had best do it during their stop. Another piece of her
petticoat offered Deborah a dry bottom for a while again.
Food was thrust at her, and she willed herself to eat it. She
had no idea what it was. It was tough and dry, but softened
in her mouth as she chewed. She thought it must be jerky.
She drank thirstily from the creek. When the command
came to remount, she had to try three times before she could
get back on her horse. The Indians stared wordlessly until
she succeeded. It was only the memory of that other woman
that gave her the surge of strength to make it.

At daylight they finally stopped. The Indians quickly staked
out the horses on lush grass near a thin stand of timber.
Nobody spoke to her. Nobody looked at her. It was as
though she did not exist. Nonetheless, she knew they saw

every move she made. If she made any kind of move to escape, they would catch her in minutes.

When they ate, they passed her a handful of the dried meat again. It almost tasted good. The Indians laid down and appeared to all fall asleep instantly. She hadn't seen them post a guard.

She lay down on the grass. She had never felt so tired in her life. The insides of her thighs were raw from riding so long bareback. Her back and legs hurt so bad she had to bite her lip to keep from screaming every time she moved. She turned over on her side and opened her blouse to allow Deborah to nurse while she lay there.

A foot in her ribs brought her instantly awake. Many Thunders stood over her. The sun was past its nadir, beginning the daily slide toward the darkness. She had slept all morning!

Deborah was sleeping contentedly in the crook of her arm. She had nursed herself to sleep.

Many Thunders spoke impatiently. "Get on horse. We go now."

She struggled painfully to her feet. She staggered to the readied horse, wishing for the courage to request a blanket. She looked around at the impassive circle of faces watching, and decided against it.

Suddenly remembering, she looked around for the two Indians Many Thunders had sent along their back trail. They were nowhere to be seen
.

She threw herself with all her strength to gain the horse's

back, and barely succeeded. As her raw legs came into contact with the horse's rough hair she started to moan. She bit it off short, so only that first syllable escaped. She closed her eyes and gritted her teeth to keep from making any more sound.

As she sat still, the first wave of excruciating pain passed. It ebbed to a hot burning pain that blended with the pain of her leg and back muscles. She opened her eyes to see that quietly mocking humor in Many Thunder's eyes as he watched her.

"What are you so smug about?" she wanted to scream at him. "Is this the way brave Indian warriors prove their manhood, by torturing women?"

She didn't say it. She kept her teeth ground together and her lips compressed to a thin, white line, waiting for him to start their travel again.

The day wore painfully on toward darkness. They stopped at another stream shortly after dark. She knew the routine now. She relieved herself, changed her baby, drank from the stream, and ate what she was offered. When the command came, she willed herself to the back of her horse again, and they continued onward.

The hours blurred into a maze of pain and shame and fatigue and fear. Her sense of modesty was lost somewhere beneath the merciless sun and before the indifferent eyes of her captors. Her grief for her murdered husband ebbed to some dull level of pain below conscious thought. Her own physical pain became the whole focus of her awareness.

She drew a curtain of determination around her. She was going to live. She was not going to die. She would not die!

Her baby was going to live. Nothing else mattered, for right now. Later, perhaps, other things would matter again. Now, there was only the insistent resolution to survive. To live. To not die. And not to cry. They would not make her cry! They would see no tears from her eyes!

Days and nights melted together in a red-tinged haze of pain and fatigue. She had no idea how far they had traveled, or what direction. She knew they had entered mountains. They climbed and climbed. The weather grew noticeably colder. The streams became rapid and noisy. The ground became rocky and the trails strewn with great boulders. Then they descended to lower foothills again, bearing always, she thought, mostly north. After the first couple of days she focused her eyes only on the horse ahead of her, and saw little else. Even that she saw through a red haze of pain and fatigue.

She thought it must have been a week of that kind of hard riding before they arrived. She first felt a change in the attitude of the Indians that morning. They too were tired. So were their horses. It was a grueling ride, even for seasoned warriors. But that morning she sensed a renewed bounce in their step. They said nothing she could understand. There was just a difference.

It was mid-afternoon when she learned why. They rode out onto a ridge that overlooked a long valley. A large stream sparkled in the sun as it wound its way through the course of the valley. There were clumps of timber that showed different shades of green. Pine. Spruce. Fir. Aspen. The silver-backed leaves of huge cottonwood trees winked along the bottom, in a few places.

The snow-capped mountains gave the valley a backdrop that made the view breathtaking. Myra gasped as the beauty of the vista penetrated her fatigue and pain. "It's beautiful!" she said softly.

Nobody answered, but Many Thunders looked at her for a long moment before he turned away. Then he pointed.

She saw the village then, maybe a little over a mile away. There must have been fifty or sixty tepees cast in some helter-skelter arrangement around a large open space. On the near side of the village a rope corral held a sizeable group of horses. As she let her eyes wander over the valley she spotted two other groups of horses grazing. Near one group she saw several figures. They were so small they looked like toys in the distance, but she assumed they were Indian herders tending the horses.

Wordlessly the group started down the ridge. At the bottom they stopped. Many Thunders motioned her forward. He made her ride to a position directly behind him. The others all fell into some position along a single-file line that they all seemed to understand perfectly.

When they were all in their proper places, Many Thunders again led out. In a matter of minutes they were parading through the tepees toward that central cleared space.

The entire village was out to meet them. The warriors held up the scalps they had taken. They had spread much of the captured booty onto their horses' backs for all to see. Many Thunders now held the reins of Myra's horse, demonstrating that she was part of the booty he had won. Words she did not understand followed them. She understood the oohs and aahs, and the clucks and murmurs of approval. They were conquering heroes, home from the wars.

Twice an Indian woman ran from the group and grabbed the

reins of a horse that bore a dead man. Twice a high, piercing, haunting wail rose above the festive scene. The wail hung in the air and echoed down the valley.

At the largest tepee, Many Thunders stopped. He pointed to the tepee, then motioned Myra down from her horse. She slid from the animal stiffly, grasping its mane with one hand and her baby with the other. By the time her legs would hold her, Many Thunders had motioned her toward the tepee again. Clouds were gathering on his brow, but she could push herself no faster.

Pushing away from the horse she staggered to the door of the tepee. An Indian woman lifted the flap for her, and she stumbled inside. She fell onto a pile of animal skins that lay on the floor. They felt soft. She had no strength to rise. She turned onto her side. She had long since given up any effort to button her blouse when she nursed Deborah. The baby reached for, and found, the nourishing and comforting taste of her mother, but her mother had already lost consciousness.

She was wakened some time later with abrupt crudity. Many Thunders hovered over her, then lowered himself onto her to claim her as his own. Roughly, wordlessly, he forced himself on her. She bit her lip until it bled, determined she would not cry out, that she would endure whatever she must endure to survive, to save herself and her baby. She slipped back into unconsciousness almost before he had finished.

§§§

Out of reach of her mind, Levi Hill sat up suddenly in his bunk. Sweat stood out on his brow. It must have been that dream again. He could no longer remember a time it did not haunt his sleep, forcing him to relive the terror of his parents' death. He wished it would just go away. Even as he framed the thought, he knew this was more than the old familiar memory, replayed as a dream.

More than a week now this new thing had haunted him. It had begun with that first cold wind that blew across his mind in the breaking corral. He rose and walked softly to the bunkhouse door, careful not to wake the other hands. He looked across the yard at the ranch house. He could be sleeping there, he knew. They treated him as the son he had never really been. He thought they loved him as a son. But he always felt like an outsider anyway. Even after Myra married and left, and there was no one living in the house except the rancher and his wife, he still preferred the bunk-house. It was a better place for an outsider.

He looked across the moonlit sage brush tiredly. He wanted so badly to go back to sleep. He also knew, if he did, the dream would come again.

"Whatever's comin' I just wish it'd get here," he murmured. He wondered later if things would have been different if he hadn't said that.

Chapter

Four

He was so intent on watching the trail he nearly missed the sudden movement of his horse's ears. As those ears sprang to attention, almost by instinct, he dove from the saddle. He heard the soft twang of two bow strings while he was still in the air.

He hit the ground and rolled to his feet as the first of the Indians leaped at him. He sidestepped and swung a booted foot below the arcing knife, catching the man in the stomach. The Indian grunted and rolled into a crouch.

Jim's gun roared, and the Indian grunted again. He sidestepped again, whirling to meet the charge of the second Indian. His gun roared again, and the second Indian dropped soundlessly to the ground.

He whirled back toward the first Indian. He was nowhere in sight.

Jim looked about frantically, backing toward his nervous horse. There was no sound. The second Indian lay without moving where he had fallen. There was no sign of the first one.

Reaching his horse, Jim stood thoughtfully. Finally he holstered his gun and removed his boots. Pulling a pair of moccasins from his saddle-bag, he slipped them onto his feet. Moving swiftly and silently, he slid through the brush. He reached a vantage point where he could see the spot the first Indian had fallen. He studied the area. Finally he spotted tell-tale blood spots revealing the path the wounded warrior had taken.

He followed the trail carefully, staying always to one side, away from any expected line of pursuit. It took him almost two hours to find him.

He was dead. He had struggled to a place of hiding from which he could watch his back trail. He had fitted an arrow to his bowstring and awaited his pursuer. The pursuit of death had found him first. Even in death his eyes remained fixed on the way he had come, awaiting the prey-turned-hunter that followed.

"What a waste o' fine manhood," Jim muttered softly. Turning, he returned to his horse. Exchanging his moccasins for boots again, he mounted his horse and continued following the trail of the war party.

A long way away, sitting at the table in the chow hall, Levi Hill realized he was holding his breath. He released it with a rush. He shook his head and busied himself in the steaming cup of coffee. Jim Keller was totally unaware of Levi's existence. Levi was just as unaware of Jim's identity.

It was the circling birds Jim next noticed. He rode in a direct line toward the carnage they flagged. He was not yet in sight of the source of their interest when he saw the woman.

She was walking slowly, looking straight ahead. She was stark naked, except for shoes and a torn dress collar, still buttoned around her neck. Her body was burned red by the sun, covered with bruises, and streaked with the reddish brown of dried blood.

She was walking southward along a shallow draw. A small stream meandered beside her. As he watched, stunned by her blank and disheveled look, she walked into the water. She seemed not to notice. She crossed the small stream and kept going, walking straight ahead. She looked to neither side. She did not blink. She gave no indication she saw Jim Keller.

He slid from his horse and stepped into her path. She kept walking, as though she did not see him. Her eyes were unfocused, staring straight ahead.

He grabbed her by both shoulders. "Ma'am! Stop!" He had no idea what else to say.

She stopped. She looked down at his hand on her shoulder, staring at it for a long moment. Then she slowly turned her head and looked at his other hand, resting on her other shoulder. She reached up and picked up one of his hands. She turned it over, then back again, studying it with a blank expression. Finally she raised her eyes and looked into his face.

A look of ineffable pain crossed her features, and they went blank again. He shook her gently. "Ma'am, you got to wake up. What happened? Where's your man?"

The eyes focused on him again. A look of unbearable terror flowed across them in an instant, then the blankness returned.

Jim stepped back. She stood still. He untied his bedroll and drew out a blanket. He threw it around her, tying it around her waist with a pigging string he drew from his saddle-bag. She looked down at the coarse blanket with an uncomprehending stare.

"Ma'am, you got to get on my horse," he told her. She gave no indication she understood.

He took her arm, pressuring her gently toward the horse. She took several steps, but stopped as soon as he stopped pulling her that way. He resumed the pressure, guiding her to the side of the horse.

"Ma'am, you got to get on that horse."

There was no response. He pushed his hat to the back of his head and tugged at his ear lobe. Shrugging his shoulders, he grasped her by the waist and lifted her to the saddle.

As she settled into the saddle, the blanket was pushed up off her right leg, exposing nearly the entire thigh. She seemed not to notice. Jim tried to pull the blanket down where it would cover her better, but she did not respond. Too much of the blanket was under and around her. He could not pull it enough to cover the exposed flesh. He gave up trying and left it that way. He set out northward, leading the horse. As they neared the top of the rise he hesitated. He looked at the nearly catatonic woman a long moment, then back at the rise ahead of them. The north breeze bore ample testimony to what he was about to find. He knew the Indians were long gone, but caution would not allow him to blunder brashly over the hill.

Finally he dropped the reins, knowing his horse would

stand. He dropped to all fours and crawled to the top of the rise, where he could survey the scene he didn't really want to see at all.

From the top of the ridge he could see two men and a child lying in the yard. He could see a hand extended through the open door of the house, but could not tell from this distance whether it was a man or a woman. The three bodies in the yard had already provided food for the collection of buzzards, crows and magpies that had gathered. He could see no sign of life.

He looked back at his horse and its silent burden. He sighed heavily. Rising, he returned and picked up the horse's reins. "Can't leave you sittin' here alone," he said. "Maybe if you can help bury your folks, it'll help, somehow."

She appeared not to see as they crested the rise and descended into the yard. He led his horse to the door of the house. It was a woman's hand he had seen. The brass of three spent cartridges lay beside her. Her scalp was gone. "What Indians scalp women?" he wondered aloud.

Jim lifted the woman from his horse, and impelled her in through the door. "Find yourself some clothes," he told her. "Get dressed."

She simply stood where he had stopped pushing her. She gave no indication she even knew where she was, or even who she was.

He grabbed her by the shoulders and shook her roughly. "Ma'am! Dag-nab it, find some clothes! Snap out of it! Get dressed."

Her eyes focused on him briefly, then drifted off again. He

shook her again, a little more roughly. "Damn it, listen to me!" he yelled at her.

Her eyes returned to his, and focused. "I'm, I'm sorry. I didn't mean to cuss. I don't never cuss. But you gotta listen to me! Find your clothes! Get dressed!"

She stared at him for a long moment. Finally her eyes moved to the far side of the room. She nodded her head numbly, and started to move toward a jumble of things strewn about the floor.

Jim turned away. He picked up the body of the woman beside the door, swinging her across his shoulders. He carried her around behind the house. He saw what looked like a grave marker part way up the hill. He carried the woman to it, affirming that was what it was. He laid her on the ground gently.

He returned to the yard, doing the same with the bodies of the two men and the child. Finding a shovel, he began the task of digging a grave large enough to accommodate all of them. It was a long, hot task. The ground was rocky and hard. Some of the rocks he unearthed were nearly too heavy for him to lift out of the hole. Finally he had the common grave deep enough to discourage predators, and he deemed it adequate.

He returned to the house. The woman had managed to dress herself. She stood in the door, looking blankly across the yard.

"We need blankets," he said to her.

She did not respond. Her hands hung limply at her sides.

She stared straight into nothing. He grasped her by both shoulders again. "Ma'am! We need four blankets."

She focused her eyes on him, but said nothing. He repeated, "Blankets, Ma'am. Four blankets."

She turned back into the house. She lifted a hand to her face and brushed it across her eyes. She nodded mutely. She gathered four blankets from the jumble of strewn possessions. Jim took the blankets, then took her by the hand. "You gotta come too," he commanded.

She allowed herself to be led dumbly around the house and up the hill to the grave site. Jim started with the dead woman from the house. He wrapped her in a blanket, then lowered her as gently as he could down into the hole. She watched, but said nothing.

He did the same for the first of the men from the yard. Again, she watched in silence.

He rolled the body of the second man onto a blanket. She made a small, choking sound. He stopped and looked at her. She was staring at the dead man's face intently. He reached out and took her by the hand, drawing her close to the dead man's body.

"Ma'am, I reckon you'd oughta say good-bye. I'm guessin' this was your husband?"

She did not answer. She stared at the dead man for a long moment. Then she dropped to her knees. She reached a hand slowly to him, touching the raw wound where the scalp had been ripped away. The birds had eaten to the skull, baring the bone, but they had not yet marred the face when they were shooed away.

She brushed a hand softly across his cheek. She made the choking sound again, and rose to her feet. She doubled her fists together, holding them against her mouth.

Jim rolled the man into the blanket and lowered him onto the others, in the bottom of the grave. Then he turned to the child. He laid the boy's body onto the blanket, then looked expectantly at the woman. As before, she dropped to her knees. She wordlessly picked up the child's body and clutched it to herself, as if silently willing life back into the lifeless form. Her eyes drifted to the top of its head. She reached a hand and softly touched the ravaged flesh where his scalp had been torn away. Fire flashed for the barest moment in her eyes. Then she laid him back on the blanket and leaned back, staying there on her knees.

Jim gently rolled the child into the blanket, then lowered him into the grave with the others. Working quickly, he shoveled in all the dirt he could scrape up. Then he rolled and lifted all the rocks he had removed into and onto the site, making a rock cairn over the common grave. That would not only mark the site, it would prevent predators from digging up the corpses as well.

Only when he had finished did he look at the woman again. She was still where she had stayed after he took the child. She was staring at the fresh wound in the earth and the cairn of rocks.

Her face began to move. Unspeakable pain abruptly twisted her features. He reached out and touched her arm. As he touched her, the woman jerked with a spasmodic sob. Another followed it. Then she broke into a loud wail of anguish that ascended to the top of the hill. It arced into the sky and echoed from the other side of the valley. The returning echo gave the wail an eerie depth, blending with the sound still issuing from her throat. It sent the wordless cry of agony into a circle of hopeless sound.

The wail lasted so long Jim moved to stop her. "Ma'am! Ma'am! You're gonna lose your breath an' die if you don't stop it now."

The wail did stop, but not abruptly. It stopped by breaking, then turning into a broken stream of sobs and unintelligible words that tumbled like water from a ruptured dike. She reached blindly for him. He reached down to her extended arms and lifted her up. She wrapped her arms around him and clung to him as though he could save her from drowning in the sea of agony sweeping over her. She clung to him and sobbed out of control for a long time.

§ § §

Many miles to the south, a ways north of Laramie, Levi Hill stood in the gate of the breaking corral at the S R Bar ranch. He brushed at a tear that was plowing a furrow down the dust of his cheek. He had no idea where it came from, or why. He was just suddenly stunned by such an overwhelming sense of grief he wanted to cry. He did cry. He had shed no tear since the day he watched his own family butchered from his sage brush concealment. He brushed the tear away hastily, looking around to be sure nobody saw it.
Then he felt an inexplicable surge of anger rise within him.

Again, he had no idea of its source. "This is gettin' on my nerves," he gritted. "What in the world's goin' on? Whatever's comin', I just wish it'd get here."

§ § §

Even as Levi seethed at his own feelings, Jim Keller was struggling with equally difficult emotions. The woman would not stop her sobbing. He did not know how long she needed to continue. He only knew how long he could tolerate sharing her unspeakable pain. He was still holding her. Her face was still buried against his chest. He finally unfolded his arms from around her. He took her again by the shoulders. He pushed her back away from him, to arms' length. He stared hard into her eyes.

"Ma'am! We got to ride! We can't do no more here. We got to get you somewhere where there's folks to take care of you. Then I got to get on after them gut-eatin' Indians. They got another woman they took with them. I got to try to get her back."

She struggled to force her sobs and wails under control. She stared at him for a long moment before his words penetrated. When they did, panic rose in her eyes. She grabbed his wrists with both hands.

"You're... You're... You're going after, after... them?" she said between the still unstifled sobs.

He nodded. "I got to, Ma'am. Is there another place somewhere's close?"

She stared at him again a long moment, clearly fighting to gather her thoughts. "There's... There's Anderson's... a couple... couple miles east," she said, still speaking with difficulty. "If... If they didn't... didn't get there too."

Jim pursed his lips. "I don't reckon they did," he said. "They been headin' right straight north. They're movin' purty fast."

He looked at the house, then back at her. "Listen, I don't reckon you'll be needin' nothin' from here right now. I'll take you over to the Anderson place. They'll bring you back for your stuff, or take care of whatever you need."

The Anderson ranch displayed careful planning for permanent residence. The house was square and solid. The outbuildings were well placed and soundly built. The corrals were orderly and strong. "Buildin' for the future," Jim murmured approvingly.

He was lying on the hill overlooking the spread. He was certain the Indians were bearing north, but he was too cautious to ride directly into the yard, nonetheless.

Finally he saw two hands emerge from the bunkhouse and head for the corral. From the relaxed demeanor of their walk, he was convinced there were no dangers lurking unseen.

The relaxed demeanor vanished instantly as the strange looking pair rode in. "That's Donna Summers!" one of the cowboys yelled.

"Andy!" the other cowboy yelled toward the house. "We got trouble!"

By the time they reached the house the rancher and his wife were on the front porch, and four cowhands were gathered close. Mrs. Anderson ran to the woman with Jim. "Donna? Oh, Donna! You look awful! Oh, Donna, what happened?" The woman fell from the horse, sobbing hysterically, into the ranch woman's arms. As Ruby Anderson helped her into the house, Jim quickly filled in the others.

"What tribe?" were the first words spoken by the rancher. "Don't rightly know," Jim admitted. "I ain't from around here, and I ain't seen none quite like 'em afore."

He described the Indians' look and dress. "Crow!" the
rancher said at once. "I was sure it wouldn'ta been Shoshone. We get along real good with them. Now what the
Sam Hill is Crows doin' down here?"

He looked into the distance absently for several seconds,
then started abruptly. "Well, now! Here I am forgettin'
every speck o' manners I own. Get down! Come in. You're
hungry, I reckon."

He was. And tired. He ate ravenously, then prepared to go.
"You aimin' to keep followin' 'em?" the rancher asked.
He nodded. "They still got that other woman. What did
you say her name was? Myra Hackett?"

The rancher nodded. "She's Stubby Rudabaugh's girl. He's
got an outfit down towards Laramie. I reckon I'll be sendin'
him word. He'll likely get you some help, if you stick
around a spell."

Jim thought about it a while, then shook his head. "I ain't
good enough at trackin' to foller 'em if'n I let too much time
go by. I'd best hang kinda close on their heels."

It was three hours from the time he arrived that Jim rode out
of the Anderson yard, heading at a fast trot to intercept the
trail of the fleeing war party of Indians. It was nearly dark
when he found it, several miles north, still heading the same
general direction. At dark he found a place to camp. He
was in the saddle again at first light.

Several times the next day he guessed at the general direction they were fleeing, and rode straight and fast without
watching for signs of their passing. Each time he found their
trail again with no difficulty.

The trail swung back to the west, and entered the mountains. "Must be avoidin' some town or fort or somethin'," he reasoned.

The trail continued to grow colder. He knew they were covering country much faster than he could, because they were riding day and night, stopping only for brief rests. He could not do so. He had to follow in daylight to be alert for more traps and ambushes. He had to see their trail. He followed them from first light until encroaching darkness made the trail too dim to see. He could do no more.

§ § §

In that distant ranch yard, Levi leaned on the top rail of the corral. His eyes strained from looking up the road. He was waiting for something. He just didn't have any idea what he was waiting for. Whatever it was, he no longer had any doubts about its coming. The cold knot that never left his stomach anymore assured him of that. It would come. He was also certain that when it came, it would not be welcome. He drew the Colt .45 from its holster and checked the loads for the tenth time.

"Still got it, huh?"

He had heard Sandy approaching. He only nodded.

"Lastin' a long time," the cowboy observed.

Levi nodded silently again. It wouldn't be much longer, though. He didn't know how he knew that. He just knew it.

Chapter

Five

Myra woke with a start. It was not really dark, but she couldn't see clearly. She had no idea where she was.

Strange smells assailed her nostrils. What she could see of her surroundings were foreign. She felt the panic of disorientation overwhelm her. She stifled the urge to scream, but her eyes kept casting wildly about.

Deborah! The baby! She was nursing her, wasn't she? Where was she?

Squinting in the semi darkness she finally saw her. An Indian woman was holding her. Thoughts stampeded through her mind.

"What is she doing with my baby?"

"Where am I?"

She moved. Intense pain shot through her legs and back. She gritted her teeth to keep from screaming.

Her mind raced. "She's nursing her! She's nursing my baby!"

She tried to get to her feet to lunge after her baby, to take her away from that terrible, dirty savage. She couldn't. Her legs refused to hold her. She collapsed back on the soft pile of furs.

She looked about wildly. Memories came rushing back. She remembered the murder of her husband. She recalled the savage gang rape of the other captive woman. The long, long ride with little rest and almost no food or water. The encampment. The memory of being raped by Many Thunders shortly after their arrival was almost lost in the haze of half-consciousness in which it had occurred. She was a prisoner! She was a prisoner of the Indians who had killed her husband!

She looked back at the woman who was nursing her baby. The woman stared back at her, without expression. She spoke. "Your baby was hungry. You have no milk. It has been too long since you ate well, or drank enough. I hope it does not offend you that I am nursing her."

Myra stared at the woman, leaning forward to try to see her clearly in the near darkness of the tepee. "You… You're… You speak English!" she said.

The woman nodded. "I am white."

"You… You are a captive too?"

"I was," the woman affirmed quietly. "That was a long time ago. My family were all killed. I was brought to the camp of this people."

"How… How long ago was that? How long have you been a prisoner?"

"I am not a prisoner. I stay of my own will. I have a husband here. I have two children here. These are my people now. My husband is Running Warrior."

"You… you… married one of these Indians?"

The woman was silent for a long while. Finally she spoke again. There was something in her voice Myra could not identify. She sounded tired. Or resigned. Or indifferent. "It is marriage, yes. It is not a Christian marriage, because these are not Christian people. But it is marriage. There are three of us who are married to Running Warrior. We share the work, so it is not so hard. He is a very good hunter. He provides well for us."

Myra could think of nothing to say. At last the woman rose and carried the full and contented baby back to her. "You must get up and move around. I put some balm on your legs, where they are rubbed raw by riding bareback. I will bring more. You will be expected to begin working in the morning. I will interpret for you, when I can. I will teach you the language. It will help you get along and adjust quicker."

A sudden realization swept over Myra. "You mean… You mean I'm going to be here for… forever?"

The dark haired woman looked at her for a long moment, without expression. "It seems frightening, I know. It is not so bad, if you do not fight. If you do what you are told, and do it quickly and willingly, you will not be treated badly. You must especially do whatever Many Thunders asks of you, whenever he wishes to have you."

"When he… what?"

"You are his woman now. You are one of his wives. That is why he would not let the rest of the war party use you. He saved you for himself."

"He… He thinks I'm… that I'm going to let him… that…"

"He has already claimed you as his woman, even though you were barely conscious. It was done openly, before the others, to serve notice that you belong to him, and to him alone. You are one of his wives now. It will only hurt you if you try to fight him, or if you refuse whatever he asks of you," the woman assured her.

She rose to leave, but Myra grabbed her. "Wait! Don't leave me! I don't even know your name. When will Many Thunders be back? Isn't there some way I can escape? Won't somebody come looking for me? I'm not going to have to be an Indian, am I?"

The woman removed her hand gently. "There is no way to escape, and nobody to rescue you. They would have no idea where to look for you. I do not know when he will want you. It is customary for a man to concentrate on his newest wife pretty heavily for a time, until he grows used to her. You are very sore, and you seem to have won his favor, and he is very enchanted by your red hair. He may be a little less demanding of you for a little while, until your legs heal and you are rested. He may not. I have no way to know."

With no further words the woman was gone. A moment later she thrust her head back into the tent. "Oh, my name is Victoria, but I have not been called by that name for a very long time. Here, my name is Runs In Beauty. I will teach you to say it in the Crow tongue."

Then she was gone. Myra clutched her child to her, frantically. Her mind whirled, refusing to light on anything for more than a fleeting instant. Like a hummingbird, it darted forward and backward, here and there, lost in a jumble of frightened and confused thoughts.

She slept again. She thought she would never dare close her eyes again, but she slept almost at once. It was daylight when she wakened.

The tepee was bustling with activity. She desperately needed to relieve herself, but had no idea where to do so. She forced herself to her feet, gritting her teeth to endure the pain. Deborah was lying near the small cook fire, naked. Beside her was an Indian baby, just as naked. They both appeared contented, so Myra resisted the urge to grab her and dress her.

She looked uncertainly toward the flap that led outside. An old Indian woman rose effortlessly from her cross-legged sitting position. She motioned Myra to follow, and went through the flap. Wordlessly, Myra followed, forcing her stiff legs to obey her will with difficulty.

The sunlight hurt her eyes, and she blinked blindly for several seconds. Finally she saw the woman who had beckoned to her, walking away between two tepees. She followed as swiftly as she could force her legs to navigate.

The woman led her to a place in the edge of the timber that smelled like it was customarily used for the purpose for which she so desperately needed it. Remembering the casual attitude of the Indians in the war party, she forced herself to attend to her needs without thought of modesty.

When she was finished, the old woman turned wordlessly and led the way back to the tepee.

The days became a maze of timeless torment. She was, as Victoria had predicted, expected to begin work at once. She had worked hard on the ranch, but this was harder than anything she had ever done. She was shown how to scrape and tan hides with the brains of the animals themselves. She was shown how to find and prepare roots and berries and leaves and bark. She was shown how to cut meat into thin strips and smoke it, to preserve it for winter's food. She was forced to work without letup from first light to dark.

She began to learn some few words of the Crow language, so she could begin to understand some of the things being said around her and to her. She made no effort to reply to any of it.

She saw Many Thunders several times each day. Almost never did he look directly at her, but she could feel his eyes possessively on her often. She avoided all eye contact with him, trying to prevent any hint of willingness on her part. It mattered not in the least. As Victoria had predicted, she received the full force of Many Thunder's desires. At least she was certain it was the full capacity of his attentions. He surely couldn't have had any energy left over for any of his other wives! Every time he came to her in the dark, he left her exhausted, nauseated and filled with loathing. His earthy and unwashed smell, his attitude and his approach were all crude and, to her, savage.

Victoria's presence was the only thing that enabled her to retain her sanity. They talked often, in hushed tones, when they could manage to be together. After the first few days, when she had assured the Indian women that Myra would not try to escape, they were allowed more freedom together.

That's why Victoria was there when Myra saw him.

They were together, picking the juicy red raspberries from along the clear stream. Their crude baskets were nearly full, and they were ready to start back. As she stretched and arched the pain from her back, Myra's eyes drifted to the rim of the ridge beyond them. As she did, a man stepped out of the edge of the trees, and just stood there where she could see him.

It was a white man who wore a hat and boots and chaps and a gun. He had a gun! He carried a rifle. He was looking right at her!

She caught her breath sharply. She whirled to look at Victoria, but Victoria could not have seen him from her position. She looked back at the man. He was gone.

She wanted to cry out. She wanted to run after him. She wanted to tell Victoria. She did none of those things. Who was he? Why did he show himself to her? Had he managed to follow them from where she had been captured? Was it just some cowboy who had stumbled onto the Indian encampment? No! If that were the case, he would not have had any interest in her. He showed himself to her! He did! He just deliberately stepped into the open, and showed himself to her. Was that to tell her someone knew she was there? Would he go get help? Did he need any help?

Her father! Her father had found out about her capture and had sent his cowboys to rescue her! Or maybe he had come himself! No! She could not bear the thought of her father in that kind of danger. The picture of her slain husband flashed in her mind again.

No, it wasn't her father. She would have recognized him. It

wasn't Levi, either. He was so distinctive with those short legs of his, she would have recognized him, too. But it might have been somebody sent by her father, or who was scouting for her father.

The thought that her father might be near sent a new course of strength through her, even as fear for him nearly choked her. He could not rescue her. She knew it. But maybe he could let the army know where she was!

A torrent of thoughts tumbled over each other in her mind. She stood, slack-jawed, staring at nothing, as they fought for some sort of order.

"What on earth is the matter, Myra?" Victoria asked.

Myra whirled. "It's… It's… Oh, it's… nothing. I just thought I saw something for a minute, that's all."

"Saw something? What? You look like you've seen a ghost."

"I… no! No. It's nothing. I just thought I caught a glimpse of a bear, and it startled me. I think we should go back. My basket is full."

She watched after that. She watched constantly, but saw nothing more. There was no indication from any of the Indians that any white man had been seen in the area at all. She watched, though. She waited. She believed.

That night she dreamed of her father. Stubby Rudabaugh was a short, red-faced rancher with a ring of red hair around a large bald spot, and a heart as big as Wyoming. In her dream, she saw a rider gallop into the ranch yard. He was met there by a boyish-looking cowboy with broad shoulders and short legs. He was the one her father had rescued after his family's wagon train had been attacked by Indians. She was younger then, but she had always been frightened by the anger and determination that smoldered in his eyes. As she watched, the young cowboy picked up a rifle and mounted a horse. The horse spread a majestic pair of wings and leaped from the ground. He began riding the wind to come to her. It was her brother! Levi! He was coming for her!

She knew he wasn't really her brother. She remembered when her father had found him, wandering alone and on foot. Because he was the only survivor of that Indian attack on the wagon train, they had taken him in. He had become the brother she never had. From the very beginning he had been fiercely defensive of her. She had felt, even when they were both still very young, that she could go anywhere safely so long as Levi was with her. He could protect her against anyone or anything. Her faith in him was boundless. It was, therefore, natural that she should dream of him, just now. His strength and his uncanny ability with pistol or rifle had been awe-inspiring since he was still a child. If anyone could find her, rescue her, it would be him.

In the dream a cowboy stood to one side, motioning to him, and pointing to her. Levi's horse flew at impossible speeds on the wind, but the cowboy didn't move. Yet the cowboy stayed always even with Levi. The cowboy was the man she had seen on the ridge. It was a dream. But it was not just a dream. She didn't know how she knew that, but she knew it.

The dream shifted, and she sat on her father's lap again. She was a small girl, snuggled in the ultimate security of the man's arms who could fix anything. His arms around her were so strong! He smelled of horses and honest sweat and safety. She smiled softly in her sleep. She didn't even notice that Levi was no longer in the dream.

Chapter

Six

Jim leaned against his horse, pressing him sideways into the edge of the high-cut bank. He held his hand over the horse's nostrils to prevent him from snorting or neighing. In every way he could, he let the horse know it was imperative for him to stand stock still and be perfectly, frantically silent. The horse sensed his panic. His eyes rolled. His ears laid back against his head. His skin quivered. He made no sound.

Keller watched the shadows cast by the afternoon sun. The line of Crow warriors rode in almost total silence, less than ten yards from where he was hidden. He forced himself to breathe slowly, evenly, silently.

He knew with deadly certainty that one sound would bring a whole passel of Indians sweeping down on him. He knew he could kill several before they could get him. He knew just as certainly he could not kill them all. His only chance to survive was to escape detection.

He was not sure, even now, why he had hidden. There was that moment of panic that surged, unexpectedly, inexplicably within him. He had stopped, the skin crawling up his spine. He had no idea what he had heard or sensed, but he had learned by bitter experience to trust his senses.

Looking about quickly, he urged his horse into a gully washed by the countless violent thunderstorms that summers brought to this country. He spotted a steep, bare bank that overhung the gully. Dismounting, he had led his horse under the overhang, then stood beside him, listening intently. He had been there almost five minutes before he heard the soft thud of unshod hooves. Moments later he saw the shadows of nine Indians, riding in silent single file. It seemed to take forever for the small band to pass. When they were gone he remained as he was for several more minutes. Then he exhaled a long, soft sigh. His hands were trembling.

"That was close, Tug," he whispered to his horse.
The horse tossed his head in relief as Jim removed the hand from his nostrils. Jim crawled to the top of the gully and lay prone for a long while, watching in all directions. He saw no indication of any other presence.

"Well, Tug," he told his horse, speaking out loud at last, "let's just tag along with this bunch and see if they're headin' to the right camp."

It had been three days since he had lost the trail of the war party that had kidnapped the woman. He continued in the direction they had last been heading, hoping to find some sign of their passing. Perhaps, if he were lucky, he might stumble onto their camp. Perhaps, if he were even luckier, he might see it before they saw him.

The passing party of Indians were making no effort to hide their trail. He followed slowly and carefully. Each time the trail led over the brow of a hill he crawled to the top before he rode across it. If he had been less careful, he would have ridden right into them.

He crawled to the top of the next ridge, over which the band of Indians had gone. As he raised his head in a clump of brush to look beyond the hill, he nearly swallowed his tongue.

An Indian was standing less than fifty yards from him, facing away. He let his breath out slowly, silently. Beyond the Indian, the others lounged on the ground. With a surge of elation he recognized one of them as the leader of the band that had taken the woman. They did not speak. Before Jim could plan his next move, a white man approached from the south. The Indians stood, watching warily.

The leader of the raiding band stepped away from the others to meet the white man. They talked, but Jim was too far away to hear what was said. Then he saw the white man remove a bundle from behind his saddle. He carefully unwrapped, one after another, several repeating rifles. From that distance they appeared to be .44-40 caliber carbines, but he could not be sure. They might have been thirty-thirties. He handed them to the Indian. Then he gave him another bundle Jim assumed to be ammunition.

Jim's face was red with suppressed anger. He had no idea who this white man was, nor why he would be giving repeating rifles to the Indians. He only knew those rifles were certain death to somebody. He looked at the watching group of Indians again, and knew he was hopelessly outnumbered. For the second time he was forced to watch in total helplessness as events transpired that would surely mean death to unknown numbers of his own people.

The white man appeared to be angry. Something the Indian had said appeared to set him off. He waved his arms and spoke loudly and forcefully. Jim couldn't make out any of the words, but the anger was unmistakable. The Indian only watched impassively as he ranted and fumed. Then he pointed and gave a single command. The white man's torrent of words stopped abruptly. He looked at the other Indians, then shrugged his shoulders. Turning, he remounted and rode swiftly away. The Indians, their reticence gone, trooped to their leader, examining their new treasures with childlike delight.

Eventually one of the rifles was given to each of the other Indians, and the leader jumped on his horse, holding his own rifle above his head victoriously. The others remounted. They all rode off, whooping and hollering their exuberance.

As before, Jim continued to follow them carefully. It was much easier now to convince himself to crawl to the crest of each hill before he rode over it.

It was in that way he first looked down into the valley of the Yellowstone River, and saw the encampment of the Crow Indians he was pursuing.

The long valley was a scene of incredible beauty. He lay in the bushes at the rim of the canyon and studied it in detail. A mile and a half above the camp, the Big Horn River and the Yellowstone River flowed together. They were far enough removed from the mountains for the river to no longer race and tumble, but it looked like a paradise for trout, and probably several other species of fish.

The grass was lush. He could see three separate groups of Indian ponies, herded by young boys, feeding on the valley's prodigal sustenance. Clumps and groves of a dozen different kinds of trees offered their protection and bounty to the valley's residents. He spotted several groups of Indian women moving about, attending to whatever business occupied them. Smoke curled lazily from cook fires, and from the center of many of the tepees. It was a scene that looked like it was taken from one of those fine books his school teacher had kept on his own private shelf.

His eyes followed the winding of the river upstream to the south and west. In the distance he could see faint smoke in the sky, marking another village several miles downstream. He swore. "Looks like I just happened to stroll into the middle of the whole Crow nation," he told himself silently. He worried about his horse, tethered over the hill behind him. He knew the horse would hear or smell the Indian horses before long. Whether he would be silent or neigh a greeting was anybody's guess.

"All I need is a couple hundred Indians chasin' me," he muttered to himself. He squirmed back off the brow of the hill and returned to his horse. Riding quickly, but carefully lest he leave tracks that would be seen, he retreated to a safer area.

Nearly five miles away to the south he found an ideal place. Nestled high on a point of land that backed up to a tall cliff, was a clump of thick timber. From its edge he could see all approach from the front. Any approach from the rear was prevented by the cliff.

"A small bunch could stand off an army here in daylight," he said approvingly.

Hidden within the stand of timber he found a good patch of grass and picketed his horse to graze. Then he sat down to think.

He tried to recall everything he had heard and learned about Indian fighting, about the army, the location of forts in Wyoming and Montana territories, and anything else that came to mind. He tried to put himself in the place of the captive woman, and imagine what she would be thinking.

"I reckon I got to get the army," he said at last. "They'll likely come a-runnin' when they find out they got a white woman captive. But that'll take a while. Somehow, I got to find her first. I got to let her know that she ain't forgot."

He sat there thinking until dark. When it was fully dark, he built a small handful of fire where it could not be seen and cooked himself some supper. Then he carefully put the fire out and went to sleep.

The next morning he rode to a place near the spot from which he had watched the camp the day before. Selecting a spot from which he could see without being seen, he settled down to watch.

He had watched for nearly four hours when he caught his first glimpse of red hair. It flashed like a flame among the bushes along the river. Instantly on full alert, he watched intently. The woman he sought was here. She was still alive, and appeared well. She was accompanied by an Indian woman. No! It was another white woman! She was dark haired, and dressed in Indian clothing, but she was white. He was sure of it. They carried baskets of some sort.

As he watched they began to pick raspberries, putting them in the baskets they had brought for the purpose. He looked the area over carefully. Selecting a spot that would serve his purpose, he slipped backward over the brow of the hill.

Moving quickly he found the clump of trees he had spotted. It was much closer to the two women. He slid silently among its cover to a spot from which he could see both of them, without being visible from any direction.

He watched as they worked, talking together. He was close enough to hear the sound of their voices, but could not distinguish the words.

"Got to be a white woman," he muttered. "They're talkin' to each other, and she ain't had no time to learn Indian talk yet."

It was another hour before he gained the opportunity he wanted. Their baskets were filled, and they had moved some distance from each other. He waited until the red-haired woman stood and arched the kinks from her back. As her eyes swept idly over the hillside, he stepped out into the open.

His skin crawled. There was a hard knot in his stomach. He kept looking about, waiting for some cry of alarm from an alert Indian he had not seen.

It seemed like a long time before her eyes passed across him. He watched her head snap back and focus on him. She had seen him! She recognized him as a white man.

He watched her look quickly toward her companion. He had no idea whether she would share her discovery, and whether the other white woman would remain silent if she did. He had no intention of sticking around to find out, either!

He stepped back into the cover of the timber and ran, crouched, to his waiting horse. Mounting, he headed south as fast as he dared.

"Closest fort I know for sure is the one we got close to whilst we was followin' them fellers," he told his horse when he dared speak aloud. "It's a long ride, but there ain't no help for that. At least she knows she ain't forgot about."

§ § §

"You say he killed two of 'em?"

In the Kitchen of the S R Bar ranch, one of the hands from Anderson's set down his cup of coffee to answer Levi.

"That's what he said. He was wearin' moccasins, so I reckon it happened like he said. He changed back to his boots afore he left."

"Well, gather up the boys," Stubby Rudabaugh ordered his foreman.

"No."

Silence invaded the room. The assembled men and Mrs. Rudabaugh looked at Levi in surprise. They said nothing. Levi began to explain. "A whole bunch would be seen and heard by the Indians while they're still miles away. We ain't got enough men to fight a whole tribe. We'd get everybody killed and still wouldn't get Myra back. In fact, the first thing that'd happen is that they'd kill her so we couldn't."

Into the silent void Levi's logic had carved, Stubby spoke softly. "You ain't sayin' we should just let 'em have 'er, are you?"

"You know better than that!" Levi responded. "It's just that one man's got a better chance of gettin' her."

"Meanin' you, I suppose?"

"I reckon," Levi sighed. "Think about it. I got no family to grieve me if I don't make it. You folks took me in when my family were all killed, and I owe you. I've trained myself every day of my life since they were killed so I could get even if I ever got the chance. I've worked at it every spare minute for more than ten years. I can outshoot any man in the country. I can whip any three men you can put against me. And I can sneak up close enough to a deer to slap him on the rump, before he even knows I'm around. And I can track a fly across bare rock by moonlight. I ain't tryin' to brag, but I believe I'm the man that's got the best chance to go get Myra and bring her back home."

There was no answer as the assembled hands struggled to find a flaw in his argument. Those who knew him were already awed by his prowess, and knew better than to argue with any assertion he had made. He continued, "Besides, Myra's like a sister to me. Since you took me to raise, you and she's been all I've had. I'll bring 'er back, or I'll die tryin'."

There was another long and painful silence. Levi's eyes traveled around the room, locking his gaze with each man in turn, but avoiding Eleanor Rudabaugh's. He couldn't bring himself to look at her. It was not a moment to remember how much of a mother she had been to him.

Finally it was Stubby who broke the silence. "How do you aim to do it?"

Even though the rancher had voiced no agreement with Levi's assertions, he knew it was decided in that moment.

"I'll ride the way they went, and pick up the trail. Somewhere along it, I'm guessin' I'll catch up with Keller. If he's as smart as he seems to be, he'll be lyin' up on a hill watchin', waitin' for some way to get Myra away from the rest, without gettin' himself killed doin' it. He'll be easier to follow than the Indians, so I'll find him. I reckon we'll just play the hand as it comes from there."

Opinions of how to proceed began to bounce around the room like errant snowflakes in a whirlwind, but Levi wasn't listening. He slipped out and walked to the barn. He saddled his horse as the cold wind of a chilling fate sent shivers down his back.

"Well, I wanted it to get here," he told himself almost bitterly. "It sure enough did!"

The only one there as he rode out of the yard later was Stubby. He handed him a bag of grub Eleanor had prepared. The rancher took off his hat and brushed a hand across the top of his head, almost devoid of its former red covering. His voice was gruff. "Boy," he said, "you been the son I never had to me. There ain't another man in Wyoming Territory I'd trust to go after my little girl single-handed. But I know you're right in what you said in there. If it can be done, you'd be the one to do it. You be careful. We'll sure be prayin' for you, night an' day. And you bring my girl home."

He nearly choked on the last words. Levi was spared the necessity of answering as the rancher whirled and strode swiftly toward the house.

Chapter

Seven

Fort Phil Kearney nestled against the eastern edge of the Big Horn Mountains. Jim's military training took in the terrain and the fort's layout appreciatively. Situated on a grassy knoll, it was impossible to approach unseen. A small creek flowing out from under the eastern wall of the stockade gave evidence of at least one large spring located within the fort itself. Other springs joined the flow, creating a substantial stream that flowed into Clear Creek some miles downstream.

Looking south from the fort's entrance he could see the sparkling waters of Lake DeSmet in the distance. Above and behind the fort the forested slopes of the Big Horn Mountains rose into the sky. A few fleecy white clouds drifted lazily in some breeze unfelt at ground level, giving the whole scene an idyllic flavor.

That appearance was not reflected by the fort's commander. "What are you asking?" the major asked in obvious disbelief. His moustache bristled as his bushy eyebrows pulled down toward it in a fierce frown.

"I don't reckon I'm askin' anything," Jim replied. His drawl contrasted sharply with the major's clipped words. "I just reckoned a white woman kidnapped by Indians was most likely a matter of concern to the army."

The major's face reddened a shade further at the inferred slur against his priorities. "I have no reports of any missing white women," he said coldly, "and no reports of any recent Indian raids. Especially by the Crow. I have nothing more than your word that the entire incident ever took place. I have nothing but your very incredible story to substantiate the notion that this supposed woman was taken to some Indian camp. A camp, I might add, that is in the middle of the entire Crow nation, by your account. And you want me to take a detachment of my soldiers, ride into that camp, and demand the return of a woman who may or may not exist?"

Jim felt his own face reddening. "Major, I got no reason to say she exists if she don't. I tol' you what I seen. I tol' you where she's at. Seems to me the army'd want to get 'er back. Seems to me there might even be some duty involved."

"Young man, let me tell you something of duty, and of the reality of the army in Indian country. We survive because we choose not to thrust ourselves into impossible and suicidal situations. If I ride into that camp with a detachment of soldiers, they will most certainly all be killed. In addition, the entire relationship between the Indians and the settlers in Wyoming Territory, as well as Montana Territory, will be thrown into jeopardy. If the Indians should again choose to go on the warpath, every homestead and ranch in the territory would be threatened."

"So you're just gonna look the other way an' let 'em have 'er?" Jim asked in tightly controlled calm.

"I'm not going to do any such thing!" the major exploded. "I am going to observe that your report is unsubstantiated, and that I have a responsibility to my command. I am going to dismiss this report and assume, until and unless I get some further corroboration, that there is no such woman to let them have. Now I have a great deal of work to do. You are dismissed."

Jim restrained his impulse to salute as he turned on his heel and walked out. The sergeant at the desk in the outer room smirked at him as he passed, but said nothing.

A settlement had sprung up to the south of the fort. He walked that direction, leading his horse. He seethed in helpless rage. He decided to seek the cool shadows of the hastily constructed saloon to contemplate the matter.

He was still seated at a table there when the sergeant from the fort commander's office walked in. He sauntered to the bar and ordered a whiskey. He tossed it down and ordered another. Holding that one, he turned and leaned backward against the bar, resting on his elbows. He looked around the room, spotting Jim almost at once.

"Well, if it ain't the Johnny Reb," he said immediately. "You and your cock-and-bull story didn't get too far with the major, did you?"

"As a matter of fact, he didn't seem too concerned that a white woman has been kidnapped by the Indians," he drawled. "But then, I've noticed most Yankee officers is just chair-polishin' jaybirds too busy scratchin' their lice to do nothin'."

The sergeant gave a short laugh. "He don't think there ever was no such white woman," he said with a grin. "He thinks one Johnny Reb what's sore over losin' a war is just tryin' to stir up a fight by dreamin' up a story about something that never happened."

"He thinks that?" Jim asked in disbelief. "Why, that whore-chasin' son of a spavined weasel!"

The sergeant's grin widened. He said with a broad and exaggerated smoothness, "He thinks you just made up the whole thing, just to get the army to ride into a whole mess of Indians and get all shot up. He thinks you just figured out a real coward's way of tryin' to get even."

Jim stood up and walked forward, stopping about three feet in front of the sergeant. He had to look up slightly, and it surprised him. He was almost exactly six feet tall, and he was not accustomed to having to look up to other men. "What do you think?" he asked the sergeant softly. "Are you the sort of a yellow-bellied boot-lickin' ring-tailed, hog-lovin' coward that'd agree with that, so you don't have to risk your yellow skin goin' after her?"

The sergeant sat his drink on the bar and stepped a short step away from it. The grin never left his face. "Why, I just have to agree with my commanding officer," he said in mocking tones. "I think you are a liar."

Blood flew from his grin as Jim's fist smashed his lip. His head snapped back, but the blow seemed to have no greater effect. He responded with a swift right hook that landed on Jim's ear, filling his head with a roaring explosion of light. Jim's second blow was right behind the first, landing at almost the same instant his ear felt the sergeant's fist. They stood there, toe to toe, exchanging blows in a furious barrage of punishment. Jim knew this was not the way to fight the big man, but he craved a mindless release for his pent-up emotions. He flailed away with reckless abandon, ignoring the damage the other's fists were inflicting on him.

He had watched helplessly too many times in the past two weeks, as others had desperately needed the help he could not give. He had cowered silently as those who had made themselves his enemies passed calmly by. He had seethed helplessly as his pleas for help were dismissed. Now he had an outlet for all the anger and helplessness, and he was not going to waste it.

The sergeant soon began to back up slightly under the ferocity of the onslaught. He threw some of his best punches at this stranger in the Confederate Army shirt, and they were totally ignored. The taunting glint in his eyes slowly gave way to respect, then to a tinge of fear.

As he took a couple steps backward, Jim felt his uncertainty and retreat. He redoubled the frenzy of his attack. The increase in number and force of the blows accelerated the sergeant's retreat.

As he took another step backward, the sergeant's boot caught the leg of a table and he fell backward. He rolled instantly to his knees and tried to lurch to his feet. He was not quick enough. While his face was still slightly more than a foot above the floor, Jim's boot caught it squarely with an irresistible rising force. It lifted the sergeant clear off the floor, turning him over so that he landed on his back.

He again rolled to his hands and knees to rise, but another kick from Jim's boot caught him in the ribs. There was an unmistakable snap of breaking ribs.

The sergeant rolled to a sitting position, grabbing his side. Jim's boot caught him on the side of the head. He toppled to the floor, where he lay motionless.

Jim turned to survey the watching patrons of the saloon. He forced himself to breathe slowly and evenly, even though his lungs were screaming for air. "Any other son of a travelin' skirt-chasin' polecat think Jim Keller's a liar?" he asked softly.

There was no response.

He walked back to the table where he had been sitting and sat down again. He was no sooner seated than a powerfully built young cowboy sat down across from him. "You suppose maybe you oughta get some o' them cuts cleaned up a little?" he asked in a calm and conversational tone.

Jim looked at him through eyes that were already threatening to swell shut. "I thought I'd sit here a while and play like that overgrown sow-suckin' whore-spawned jackass never hurt me none, first," he said.

The other man chuckled appreciatively. "You got your work cut out for you," he observed. His voice was dry with exaggerated nonchalance. "You look like some old she-wolf chewed you up and drug you home for her pups."

Jim grinned, then winced as the movement hurt his battered mouth. "Thet sow-suckin' son of a three legged bobcat did sorta mark me up, didn't he?"

"He did for a fact. Do you always cuss like that?"

"Cuss? I don't' cuss atall. My ma, she wouldn't never stand for cussin'. Raised us boys as Christians, she did."

"Well, maybe you don't use any cuss words, but you sure do a lot of cussin' without 'em."

The battered face broadened its painful grin. "You oughter hear me when I get wound up."

"I'd just as soon not. It might be catchin'. I got a tent pitched over by the crick. Why don't you come over there and let me clean you up some?"

With only a moment's hesitation, Jim rose from his chair. The two walked out the door together.

An hour later, his wounds cleansed and filled with some foul-smelling salve the cowboy said would heal them, they began to talk. "My name's Levi Hill," he began. "What's that the army fella was sayin' about you knowin' some woman the Indians took?"

Jim told him the story, including the army's unexpected refusal to help. The cowboy chewed the matter over for a long while. "Well," he said finally, "I wasn't giving too great of odds that I could catch up to you this quick, but here we are."

"Catch up with me?" Jim drawled in surprise.

Levi nodded. "I ride for Stubby Rudabaugh. The fact is, he sorta raised me. He's got a big spread north of Laramie. The woman you been followin' is his daughter. She got married, and they homesteaded a ways off there. They were doin' just fine till them Indians came along."

Jim was obviously confused. "So where is this Rudabaugh?" he asked
.

Levi studied him. "He's home, waitin' for me to bring his girl back."

Jim looked at him again. It made no sense. This cowboy
looked scarcely more than a boy. His face was fresh and
round. His too-big hat made him appear like a schoolboy.
His shoulders were broad and his chest was massive, but
he couldn't have stood more than five feet eight inches. His
legs were almost comically short.

"Why would he send you?" Jim asked abruptly.

Levi hesitated. He had told his boss and foster father of
the strange and inexplicable things that had gone on in his
mind before the rider came with the news of the Hacketts.
He wasn't anxious to tell anyone else. He wasn't sure he
believed it himself. He was certain he was destined to be the
one to go, and he had convinced Stubby of the fact.
Finally, he said, "One reason, I 'spect, is he knows a bunch of
cowboys will be spotted by the Indians and killed right off.
So would soldiers. The major's right, you know."

Jim bristled. "Right? Right to just leave that woman to those
Indians?"

"Right not to get a whole unit of his army killed and start
another Indian war," Levi insisted.

"So is that what you've come to do too?" Jim asked bitterly.
"Are you going to let them rat-eatin' hair stealers have her
too? Are you going to decide there's no choice?"

"That's not exactly what I had in mind," Levi responded
calmly. "It just sounds like you and me are just gonna have
to go get her ourselves, if there's gonna be any chance at all."

Jim's eyebrows shot up. "I ain't shore I foller you. I don't
think we'd have a chance, just two of us. If'n we could hit
just the right time, maybe we could, but that'd take some

doin'."

"Worth a try, though," Levi asserted. "Any more than two of us will attract attention. Between us, we just might have a chance."

"You mean you'd tie into that whole bunch o' Indians just to help me?" Jim asked, surprise and disbelief evident in his voice.

"Nope," Levi said flatly. "I wouldn't. I trailed you all the way across the east end of Wyoming to get Myra back from the Indians, not to help you. She's my boss's daughter, but she's also the closest thing to a sister I got. This is something I just gotta do. It is not my intention to help you do nothin'. I'd be obliged for your help gettin' her, but only if you'll agree to do it my way, and do what I tell you. I know Indians some, and how they think. But I can't be arguin' with somebody when the chips are down. If we go after her together, I want it understood I'm in charge. I'll also be askin' you to talk decent. You may say you ain't cussin with that lingo o' yours, but it's cussin' as far as I'm concerned. I'm a God-fearin' Christian, an' I won't have it."

Jim stared at this boyish looking stranger in total disbelief for a long interval of silence. When he spoke, his voice was quiet. "An' if I won't do it thet way?"

Levi shrugged as if it were no great moment. "Then I'll go by myself."

Jim pondered the thought for several more minutes. Finally he said, "Fair enough. I'm a pretty fair Indian fighter, but I ain't never tangled with these. You're in command. I'll even try to leave off my lingo. But I ain't promisin' no slips! When do we leave?"

"Now's as good a time as any," he responded. "Can you ride?"

"I reckon I can ride better today than I'll be able to tomorrow," he observed wisely.

It was less than an hour later when the two rode out together, heading northeast. There was no further conversation between them. Jim's mind was totally occupied with nothing but his grim determination to stay in the saddle.

Levi's eyes were hard and flat, his lips compressed together. He made no effort to talk. The cold wind of ominous portents no longer blew down his spine. Now it settled in his stomach as a cold, hard knot. If he had felt like wondering, Jim could not have seen anything of the memories that played behind those alert, cold eyes.

Chapter

Eight

It was the worst day yet. They buried five of the Indians that day. With each warrior who died, they buried his weapons and the headdress his bravery had earned. The women were buried in their finest clothes, but with no possessions. Each child was given a favorite toy. A mound of dirt was built up over each grave.

There were the same strange, haunting chants and wails Myra had heard for the past several days. Every day it was more. The Indians called it a dying time. She knew very well what it was. It was smallpox. She did not have the words to tell them. She wasn't sure she wanted to tell them. They seemed to think it was some punishment sent from the gods. She thought that was an appropriate idea. If there were justice in this world, surely some such punishment must be given.

She struggled with her own feelings. Having had cowpox as a youngster, she knew herself to be immune to the deadly disease. She was, however, worried for Deborah.

She had no sympathy for the Indians. Something within her

delighted with the appearance of the pocks and the fevered flush on each new victim. When it was one of the men in the war party that had captured her, she almost gloated. But when the children began to die with it as well, she felt herself torn between feelings of vengeance and compassion. She had learned many things of the Indians' way of life quickly. The coaching of Victoria had helped. She had learned they lived by a stern and strict code. It was foreign to her, but they adhered to their own code more carefully than the white people she had known adhered to theirs. That was true of herself as well. She had been raised to be Christian. Even so she had often done things she knew were wrong, and had not let her Christian convictions get in her way. She only tried not to get caught.

She watched the Indians around her carefully avoid anything that violated the code of conduct that governed them. She had begun to respect them, even as she languished in the throes of captivity. She hated them because of what they had done to her and to hers. She despised them, especially Many Thunders, for his ongoing abuse of her. But she saw things in them she very unwillingly had to admire and appreciate. As the plague of smallpox spread through the village, her feelings of ambivalence increased. She began to do the things she knew would relieve the symptoms, and sometimes save the victims. She was gratified when the fevers of several broke as a result of her efforts, and she knew they would survive.

They were more than three weeks into the daily deaths when Victoria slipped hurriedly into the tepee where Myra was tending a sick child.

"Myra, you must go! You must try to run!" she said breathlessly.

"What? Why? I can't. They would just catch me. What's the matter?"

"Take Deborah and run!" Victoria repeated. "Now! Don't even wait for dark!"

She started to say something further, but was cut short by the flap of the tepee swinging wide. Daylight flooded the interior. Brings Plenty, the medicine man of the village, stood framed in the doorway, flanked by two warriors. He said something in the Indian tongue.

Victoria looked at Myra. She spoke with difficulty. "He... He says for you to come. He wants you to bring your baby, too."

"What? Why? What is he doing?"

"I... He... They have..." She whirled and ran from the tepee, scurrying past the spiritual leader of the village without looking at him.

Myra rose uncertainly. The medicine man pointed at her tepee, several yards away. He repeated what he had said before. Myra was beginning to recognize enough Indian words to know Victoria was right in what she had told her. What she didn't know was why they wanted her and her baby.

An Indian woman brushed in and picked up the sick child she had been tending. Taking the child, she quickly left the tepee. She made no effort to communicate with Myra, or with anyone else.

Myra stumbled uncertainly to the tepee that had become her

home since her captivity. She shared it with Many Thunders and his other two wives. Deborah was asleep. She had adopted the Indian custom of leaving babies totally unclothed in warm weather until they were trained, so it was necessary to wipe her dry as she picked her up. She grabbed a blanket and wrapped her in it as she hurried back out the doorway.

The medicine man and the two warriors were waiting without expression. As she emerged he motioned her to follow and turned away, walking swiftly.

As they approached the river she saw that most of the village was already assembled there. They were gathered in a circle around a large fire. Several of the stricken members of the tribe were wrapped in blankets and laid between the assembled villagers and the fire. Some of them shivered in the chills of fever. A drummer beat a staccato rhythm, and chanters kept time to it. Myra could understand no words in the chant. It sounded to her only like a repeated sound of "He –ey, ya, he-ey, ya, he-ey, ya."

She looked around for Victoria, but could not see her. She saw Many Thunders, and several others whose names she now knew. Many Thunders held the shiny repeating rifle that he was no longer seen without. She wondered idly, for the hundredth time, where he had gotten it. She had gotten glimpses of a couple others in the village as well.

She looked around at the Indians whose names she now knew. As always at important and significant times, their faces were without expression.

As she approached with the medicine man, carrying her baby, a murmur rippled around the assembled villagers. Many Thunders separated himself from the crowd and came to stand at her side. He said nothing. He did not look at her. The medicine man began a chant in a high, haunting voice. He walked a circle around the fire with his arms spread upward, gesturing at regular intervals, chanting continuously.

The other chanters had stopped. There was no sound except the drum and the old man's strange, mystic incantation. Myra felt the skin crawl along the back of her neck. A sense of immediate and overpowering evil pressed down palpably on her. The sound of the chant seemed to weave some unseen web around her, drawing her eyes and mind to the fire. From within the fire itself, a sense of darkness seemed to her to be crouched, reaching out for her. She shuddered. As the medicine man made his sixth revolution around the fire he turned toward her and Many Thunders, and said something. Many Thunders replied, then turned to Myra. "You give him baby now."

"What? Why?"

"It is the baby that has brought the spotted death to the village of my people. The blame for the dying time is mine. It is not good to bring a white baby into the village of the Crow. It is I who have done this thing. Because my heart was drawn to you, I have brought shame and death to my people. The gods are angry. It is only the spell of the medicine man that will make the gods take the death away. He must have the baby. It is part of the ceremony. It must be."

"Will... Will... He'll give her back, won't he?"

Many Thunders looked at her impassively. She could read nothing at all in his face or eyes. Finally, he said, "She will be put back into your arms when the cleansing has been made."

Reluctantly Myra held her baby out to him. He opened the blanket and picked up the naked baby, leaving the blanket in Myra's hands. He handed her to the medicine man.

The baby started to cry, but her cries were drowned out by the sounds of the medicine man as he resumed the eerie chant. Myra felt as if her feet had grown roots, holding her to the ground. She watched as in a dream she could not control. She could not wake up. She could not speak. She could only watch as if from some distant point, as though it were not her own flesh and blood the Indian medicine man held aloft.

He held the infant at arm's length above and slightly in front of him, toward the fire. He continued the chant as he shuffled sideways, making a complete circuit around the fire. When he had completed the circle he stopped, but the chant continued without interruption.

While Myra stood transfixed, a knife appeared in the Indian's hand. There was no hesitation. There was no change in his expression. He reached toward the baby with the knife. It drew swiftly across the baby's throat. Blood spurted in a crimson fountain that arced toward the fire. The baby's cries were cut off instantly. The medicine man resumed his shuffling gait around the fire, holding the child so her severed arteries pumped her life's blood in surging spurts into the greedy crackling flames.

By the time he had completed another circuit of the fire, the flow of blood has ceased. The child lay pale and lifeless in his hands. He held her aloft, as high as his hands could reach. The tone of his chant changed.

The changing of the chant seemed to loose the unseen bonds that had held Myra transfixed. She screamed. She lunged toward her baby, but was stopped in mid-stride by the iron grip of Many Thunders as he grabbed both her arms. She jerked and struggled and screamed, but she might as well have been in a vice of steel. She could not so much as gain an inch toward the lifeless body of her little girl.

The medicine man's chant ended. A deep silence settled across the scene. He turned and walked back to where Myra struggled in the Indian's grasp. He held the lifeless body of the baby out to her. He spoke.

Many Thunders responded, then spoke to the struggling woman. "He says it is a great thing to save lives. It is an even greater thing to give one's own to save the lives of a village. You will be honored as a great woman among us when the curse of the gods is now lifted. He says you must have time now to mourn. When you have mourned, you may bury your child in the way of your people. Then I will make a child in you to take its place."

He released her. She nearly fell with the sudden removal of the restraint. She grabbed the lifeless body of her child from the old man's arms. She brushed the hair from her face. She wiped frantically at the blood, cringing from the gaping slash across her throat.

She fell to her knees, unable to stand. She made no sound. She held her baby. She brushed at the blood, already beginning to dry. She rocked back and forth, clutching the child to her breast. She made no sound.

The assembled village left. They did not speak. They picked up their sick and carried them. They walked carefully around the circle of her grief. They offered no words, no gestures, no touch. They all just walked silently away. After several minutes, Myra stood, clutching her baby tightly. She walked to the bank of the river. She laid the tiny body gently on the gravel at the river's edge. She dipped a corner of the blanket in the cold water. Using it as a wash cloth, she carefully washed away all traces of the blood, rinsing the blanket's corner periodically in the river's flow.

When the baby was washed clean from head to toe, she used the rest of the blanket to dry her carefully. Then she wrapped the child's body tightly in the same blanket, and picked her up. Clutching the precious bundle against herself, she began to walk along the river's bank, upstream, toward the south and west. She either did not see, or did not care about the one Indian warrior who trailed behind her. He did not speak. He did not interfere. He only kept her in sight, following silently.

She shed no tears. She spoke no words. Even her moccasin clad feet on the rocks beside the river made no sound.

Chapter

Nine

"There ain't nobody out huntin'," Levi said softly. "There ain't any women working on skins. They ain't smokin' fish. They ain't doing anything."

"It does look unnatural quiet," Jim agreed.

The two lay in the edge of a thick clump of brush, near the top of the ridge overlooking the Indian encampment. They had ridden five days. It would normally have been three hard days from Fort Phil Kearney, along the eastern edge of Wyoming's Big Horn Mountains, but the injuries from Jim's fight had slowed them. They had narrowly escaped detection and capture by a band of Sioux. They had tangled with a group of outlaws, intent on stealing their horses.

It was that encounter that had provided them with the extra horse they hoped to need. They had totally neglected to think about what the captive woman would ride if they could effect her rescue. After they had tangled with the outlaws they thought of it. They kept the best one of their horses, turning the others loose.

They had arrived, unscathed and undetected. Now all they had to do was walk into a village smack in the middle of the Crow Nation, convince a closely guarded woman with a young baby to be quiet enough when she saw them to accompany them secretly, get her away from the Indians, then outdistance the pursuit that was certain to be launched immediately.

"We gotta be crazier'n a pair of pet coons," Jim muttered.

"What's that?"

"Crazier'n pet coons, that's what we are," Jim affirmed again. "This here's the dumbest thing two idiots ever tried to do in this world."

"It's your idea to be here," Levi reminded him. "You was following her a long time before I caught up with you."

"There!" Jim whispered suddenly. "That's her!"

Even from this distance, the flaming gold of her hair stood out like a burning flare among the dingy tepees. They watched her walk half-way across the village and disappear into a tepee

"Seems to be movin' around the village without a whole lot of trouble," Levi observed.

"Somethin's goin' on," Jim interrupted.

Several Indians moved out of their tepees and began some activity near the river's edge. It was too far for the pair to distinguish what they were doing until the smoke began to rise.

.

"They're buildin' a fire!" Levi exclaimed. "A big one. They're gettin' ready for some kind of ceremony."

"We're too far away," Jim lamented.

"We got to go around."

"What?"

"We gotta back outa here and go around where we can see what's goin' on."

"You mean where they're fixin' to have that ceremony?"

"Yup. They'll be all intent on what's happenin'. We oughta be able to get close enough to see'n hear. We might even have a chance to grab her while they're all intent on somethin' else."

"There ain't much cover down there."

"There's enough."

The two squirmed quietly back through the bushes and crawled back over the brow of the hill. Returning to their horses they rode straight away from the village. When they thought it was far enough, they swung westward. They rode clear to the edge of the river, then began following it back toward the village.

They had ridden for a full hour when Levi stopped. "We'd best tie up the horses in this bunch of brush and go on afoot."

They tied the three horses firmly, then set out. Both men

replaced riding boots with the moccasins they carried in their saddle bags. The pair moved as soundlessly as twin shadows, scurrying from bush to bush along the brushy bank of the river.

They were still a thousand yards from the towering spire of flame and smoke when a sound spun them both around. An Indian stood, arrow nocked in his bowstring, less than twenty feet from them.

A .44 appeared as if by magic in Jim's hand. A large Bowie knife appeared just as quickly in Levi's hand. Both held their ground, confused by a strange look on the Indian's face.

He stood there, looking at them, for several seconds. He made no effort to finish drawing back the arrow that he had obviously meant to send into one of their backs.

His eyes lost their focus. He stumbled forward and went to his knees. As his knees touched, Levi had traversed the distance between them. He drove the knife deeply into the Indian's chest.

The Indian fell slowly sideways, but made no sound. Levi stepped back quickly, a strange look flashing across his face. He turned suddenly ashen. He looked at his bloody knife. He whirled to a thick clump of grass and hastily began rubbing and scrubbing the blade clean.

Jim holstered his gun slowly. He watched wordlessly as the boyish-looking cowboy agitatedly cleaned and re-cleaned his knife blade. Only when the shaken Levi returned to his side did he understand. Levi spoke quietly, but with a tight edge to his voice.

"Smallpox! He was pertnear dead with it, or he'da had one of us."

"Smallpox! That's what's goin' on in the village!" Jim whispered back.

"That's what this fire's for, too," Levi affirmed. "Probably some ceremony the medicine man's gonna use to try to get the Great Spirit to take the disease away."

They resumed their stealthy approach. They found a spot nearly three hundred yards away where they could see and hear what was going on, while remaining unseen.

The medicine man was chanting something that made chills run up and down Jim's body. He wanted to ask Levi about it, but dared not speak. He craned his neck to see what was happening.

The medicine man had a baby. It was a white baby! It had to be Myra's baby. There she was! She was standing beside an imposing Indian. She was staring at the medicine man as though she were in some kind of trance.

As they watched, they saw the medicine man's hand swing in a close, swift arc. A stream of red spurted from the baby, arcing into the flame of the huge fire Jim gasped. "He killed the baby," he whispered incredulously. "He cut its throat!" His gun was in his hand. He did not know how it got there. His wrist was held in the iron grip of the incredibly strong young cowboy. "Be still!" the younger man whispered urgently in his ear. "You can't do anything now but get us both killed! If they hear us they'll be all over us like fleas on a dog!"

Jim was trembling violently. He knew the man was right. He also knew the baby was dead in spite of anything they could possibly do, even if the Indians were suddenly spirited away somewhere. He forced himself to holster his gun, but he could not force himself to stop trembling.

Levi was whispering in his ear again. "These are Crows. The one that seems to've claimed Myra is either a chief or a powerful man in the village. They'll likely leave her alone to mourn. That's a custom they have when a child dies, so it'll likely hold for this too. That might give us a chance to get her away. But we gotta wait."

The wait was excruciating. They watched as the Indians left the site in total silence, leaving the red-haired woman bent over the lifeless body of her baby. They watched her go to the river and wash the tiny corpse, tenderly wrapping it. Twice Jim started to go to her, but Levi's insistent grip on his arm restrained him.

Now the woman picked up the carefully wrapped baby and started to walk along the river. She was walking toward them!

Levi gripped his arm, pointing urgently. About twenty yards behind the woman, a single Indian warrior followed her. Signaling silently, Levi slipped away to circle around behind him.

Jim's attention was all on the woman. She was not crying. She was not speaking. She was not looking in any direction. She was just walking upstream, along the edge of the river, straight toward him.

Trembling, Jim waited until she was exactly between him

and the river. Then he stepped out of the bushes, directly into her path.

She stopped abruptly. She looked at him blankly. He spoke. "Ma'am? Myra? We've come for you. We'll take you away from here."

She looked at him for a long moment. "I saw you," she said softly.

"What?"

"I saw you. On the ridge. You let me see you."

He nodded as understanding flooded him. "I... I wanted you to know you wasn't forgot. I couldn't get to you. I was goin' to get the army."

"You didn't get them."

"They wouldn't come."

"You came anyway."

He nodded. "I had to. I couldn't just let them have you."

"You came too late."

"What?"

"You came too late. My baby is dead. They killed her."

"I know. We couldn't get there in time. I didn't know what they was gonna do till I seen what he done."

Levi reappeared as if by magic at Jim's side. He was wiping

the blade of his Bowie knife again.

"C'mon, you two," he whispered urgently. "You can talk when we've put some country behind us."

Myra looked at Levi, recognizing him with a start. "Levi! How did you get here? I dreamed of you. Where's Daddy?"

"I convinced him to let me come alone," Levi responded, the urgent note still in his voice. "I'll tell you all about it later. Now, let's move!"

"Are Daddy and Momma okay?"

"They're fine. Worried sick about you is all."

Jim never took his eyes off the woman. "We best hurry," he said.

It felt so strange and foolish to Jim. They were talking within a stone's throw of more than a hundred Indians. She was clutching her carefully wrapped baby that had just been murdered. He had followed her for hundreds of miles. She had endured incredible pain, humiliation, hardship and deprivation. And they were chatting like it was a summer picnic.

Suddenly a sense of panic overwhelmed him. He grabbed her by an arm. "C'mon!" he whispered hoarsely. "We gotta get outa here. Fast!"

They ran then. They ran from bush to bush together, back to the place the horses were tethered. There was no outcry. They saw nobody. The horses were exactly as they had left them.

Jim untied the horse they had brought for Myra. She looked at it uncertainly, then looked at him. She said, "Will you hold my baby while I get on?"

He took the lifeless form, already growing stiff, and held it gingerly. She mounted easily and reached for the body. He handed it to her wordlessly. She held the baby with both hands, letting the reins be held between a hand and the child. Her face showed no expression.

Jim mounted quickly. Levi was already leading the way to a shallow draw that led away from the river. They descended to the gravel bottom of it, then followed it, riding quickly. As soon as they were well out of sight of the Indian village, he emerged from the draw and set out straight across country, riding at a swift trot. Myra's horse followed without instruction. Jim brought up the rear, watching almost constantly over his shoulder for signs of the pursuit they all knew would come.

Levi felt an exhilarating thrill surging within him. It had eclipsed the cold hard knot of apprehension. He felt incredibly light in the saddle. His vision was so sharp he could see details of the terrain nearly a mile away. He could hear Jim's and Myra's breathing, so sharp was his sense of hearing. He was alive.

That was the word. Alive! He was in greater danger than he had been since the day his family was massacred, but he had found Myra and he could protect her now. He had walked into the middle of the Crow Nation and taken her out. He was doing what he was destined to do. He was meant to live in constant danger, to accomplish things no other man could do. His character had been forged in the crucible of violence and death. He knew it with a certainty he could neither understand nor explain. It was his destiny, he had found it at last, and it felt wonderful!

Chapter

Ten

The trio rode as though it were the devil himself who pursued. It might as well have been. They rode in silence. They rode into the westering sun until they reached the mountains, then swung south along trails that Levi seemed to know by instinct. They rode when it grew too dark to see where they were going, and nobody suggested they stop. They were still in the saddle as the sun came up.

They stopped briefly at each stream they crossed, to drink and let the horses drink, and to relieve themselves as necessary. Then they rode on.

It was late the next afternoon before they reached a spot Levi considered safe for them to stop and rest. "We'll picket the horses out and eat and sleep a while," he said. "Then we'll keep on movin.'"

They had done so. Jim fixed the bedroll from the captured horse for Myra, a little apart from him and Levi. With a great deal of difficulty, Levi persuaded her to relinquish the body of her baby. He laid it gently with their saddles, knowing by instinct that she needed to begin separating herself from it. He had to almost pull her to her bedroll and get her to lie down. He covered her gently, and walked away. Her eyes remained open. She still had not spoken since the strange conversation beside the river.

Jim went to sleep almost at once. It was dark when he opened his eyes. Myra was standing beside him. He started from his blankets. "What's the matter, Ma'am?" he asked softly.

"I... It... I don't want to be over there," she said hesitantly. "It's too far away."

"I'll move your blankets over here, if'n you want," he said.

"I want... I... Would... Would you please hold me?" she said.

He held out his arms and she rushed into them. She clung wildly to him, as though she was suddenly terrified of something. She began to tremble. He didn't know what to do. He just tightened his arms against her trembling.

From his blanket, Levi watched silently. He understood her need. He had held her that way once. She was twelve when her favorite horse was killed in a freak fall. She had remained stoic and wordless as they left the dead animal. Even later, as they explained to her parents what had happened, she had controlled her emotions. It was a day later, when she and Levi were doing chores together, that she had allowed her grief to vent itself. He had held her then, as she sobbed out her sorrow and her child's love of a favorite horse. He hadn't said anything. He didn't know anything to say. He just held her, and let her sob and cry and talk. He remembered now how strong and grown-up he had felt that day. It was the only time since his own family had been killed that he really felt he belonged to someone. She was fully his sister, if only for those few moments. She had felt so small and helpless in his arms that day, and he had vowed that he would never allow her to be hurt like that again. Now that vow was broken. She had been hurt that badly, and worse. Much worse. He had rescued her, but the hurt was already done. Deep within, he felt that was why Myra sought out Jim in this hour of need, instead of him. She went to arms that had not failed to protect her.

Except for that one time, when her grief over that horse had drawn him into the family circle, he had always been an outsider. At no other time was he ever really her brother. He didn't even question it, then, when she now reached out to a stranger instead of him in her need. It did hurt, though. He saw her jerk suddenly, like something surged within her, but she made no sound. Then she jerked again, and a choked sound escaped her lips. Then the dam of her emotions ruptured. She began to sob, great heaving sobs that shook her whole body.

Jim could feel the front of his shirt, where her face was pressed, soaked with moisture before her sobs began to subside. He made no effort to release her, or to stop her. He knew her need to cry.

When her sobbing finally began to subside he gently lowered her to his blankets. Lying down with her, he pulled the blankets over both of them together. She clung to him momentarily, then began to relax. He thought she might be able to sleep, if she would continue to accept the comfort of his arms. He himself was asleep in less than a minute. He was only vaguely aware of Levi spreading another blanket across the two of them. He didn't see the tender way Levi brushed a tear-soaked strand of hair back from her cheek.

When he woke the sun was nearly up. Myra was still asleep on his arm. It was numb to the touch, and hurt severely when he pulled it from beneath her. She did not stir as he tried to work some circulation back into the aching limb.

He let her sleep as long as possible, then woke her as Levi finished the preparations for a quick breakfast. They were in the saddle before the bottom of the sun kissed the horizon good-bye and left on its daily westward trek.

That day she began to talk. Riding close beside Jim, still clutching the dead body of her baby, all the fears and pain and tangled emotions of her whole ordeal spilled out. Jim didn't want to hear it, but Levi kept signaling him to let her talk. He knew she had to get it out of her. Levi kept actively encouraging her to talk, and Jim listened, unable to close his ears to any of it.

She stopped to cry often, then resumed again. Jim marveled at the strength and resilience of this amazing woman. "No wonder Many Thunders wanted her," he said to Levi as Myra was behind a clump of brush relieving herself.

Levi nodded. "She always was mighty special," he said. "I always figured Tom Hackett got the best woman in the territory."

The following day she finally consented to allow the baby to be lashed behind the saddle with her bedroll, so she didn't have to hold her all the time.

It was the fourth day of travel when they were sure they were being followed.

"They're comin'," Levi said.

"I seen 'em," Jim agreed.

Myra said nothing.

The three sat their horses, watching their back trail. Looking almost like ants in the distance, they counted eleven Indians, riding swiftly along their trail.

"They'll kill their horses, ridin' 'em that hard," Jim observed.

"Won't matter to 'em," Levi offered.

"Why are they still following us?" Myra asked.

"Now that's right hard to figure, if you ain't Indian," Levi said, frowning. "Might be he's just that smitten with you. Might be they all figure their manhood's been damaged, 'cause someone walked right into their village and stole you back away from 'em. Might be they just plain don't like to lose."

"Might be some of all of it," Jim agreed. "Many Thunders shore must've took a likin' to you, though, Ma'am. From what Levi tells me, it's a mighty rare thing fer one of 'em to take a woman with a baby home to be his own, and make the rest leave 'er alone on the way."

"I think he actually thought he was treating me well," Myra agreed. "He did save me from the same fate as that other poor woman. It just never seemed to occur to him that it should make any difference that he killed my husband and took me prisoner. It will surprise him if they catch up to us, and I get the privilege of letting him watch me put a bullet between his eyes!"

"They're a different people from us," Levi said. "They don't think like we think. We best find a place to make a stand."

"Can't we outrun them?"

"We ain't so far," the cowboy replied, "and our horses are tired, and so are we. They'll catch us. We best let 'em catch us where we can stand 'em off."

"That old buffalo waller wouldn't be bad," Jim observed. Levi studied the spot he pointed out. A huge depression had been worn into the ground by countless buffalo, rolling in some long-since dried up mud hole. It offered concealment, and an open field of fire, almost devoid of anything but short buffalo grass in all directions.

Levi and Jim looked at each other until a silent agreement passed between them. They both drew their rifles from their saddle scabbards, and checked the loads. Levi was pleased to see Myra pull the dead outlaw's rifle from the scabbard of her saddle and check it as well.

They looked at each other again, then at Myra. "Let's do it," Levi decided.

They moved quickly to the center of the depression. Forcing their horses to lie down, they tied three feet on each together, to keep them from standing. They could neither be seen nor shot as long as they remained prone.

Myra took her place along with them, holding the rifle that had been in her saddle scabbard, extra ammunition spread out beside her. They watched the approaching band of Indians.

They rode straight along their trail, without appearing to even look to discern it. "I shore thought we did a better

job'n that o' hidin' our trail," Jim complained.
"Ain't even slowin' 'em up, is it?" Levi chimed in with the complaint.

As the group of Indians approached, Jim found himself trying to hold his breath. He forced himself to breathe regularly, slowly. Scenes from other battlefields flashed across his mind. He remembered countless screams of wounded and dying men. He remembered the mingled smells of gunpowder and dust and smoke and blood and fear.

"Pick a target, and all fire on three," Levi's whisper interrupted his thoughts.

The approaching Indians were oblivious to their presence, thinking themselves still farther behind their quarry. They were less than a hundred yards away. Seventy five. Fifty. "One, two, three," Levi counted.

Three rifles barked in a single roar. Three Indians pitched off their horses. The rest disappeared. They just disappeared, leaving riderless horses standing and milling in confusion. "Where did they go?" Myra asked.

"In the grass," Levi answered. "Watch sharp. If you see grass moving, shoot at it. They'll crawl right up in your lap before you see 'em."

The men left Myra to watch that side of the approach. They spread out to try to watch the approaches from all other directions, knowing the Indians would circle.

Levi fired at a clump of grass that moved, and was rewarded with the unmistakable "thwack" of lead tearing into flesh. Then there was silence. There was no breath of air. Gnats swarmed in front of their faces. Sweat trickled across cheeks and down their backs. There was no sound.

Levi knew exactly what would happen. They would hear nothing. They would see nothing. Then, suddenly, screaming Indians would materialize from several directions at once. If they could shoot quickly enough, straight enough, then maybe…

They all strained to see motion in the grass. A wayward breeze rippled across the grass, and all three jerked rifles to their shoulders, then returned to their intent staring.
Their eyes began to burn from the intensity with which they watched for their own approaching deaths.

"We got company!" Jim said urgently.

Levi darted to his side to look. A large band of Indians had emerged on the hill behind them. He grinned. "Shoshoni!"

"Is that good?" Jim asked, visibly confused.

"Good for us," the young cowboy responded. "Bad for them. It's exactly why I was trying so hard to get this far south before they caught up to us. Shoshoni and Crow are like cats an' dogs."

The horses the Indians had left at the first shots had wandered off some little ways, and begun cropping grass. As Jim turned and looked, they were all gathered together. "The horses!" he yelled.

Even as the others turned to look, Indians appeared as if by magic from the grass and leaped to the backs of the horses. A wild chorus of yells erupted from seven surviving throats at once. The horses lunged to a dead run in three jumps, and the Indians rode away in a cloud of dust.

Just as they did, one Indian wheeled his horse back and stopped for an instant. Neither man had seen Myra step to the rim of the buffalo wallow and stand up. As the Indian stopped and turned back to look at her, the rifle at her shoulder barked. The Indian jerked. He stared at her for what seemed like several seconds, then turned his horse to ride away. A few feet later he toppled from it onto the ground. The riderless horse ran in pursuit of its fellows.

The leader of the band of Shoshone approached them rapidly. As he neared, Levi's grin widened. "Well now, would you look at that! You folks are just about to meet the best Indian Chief in the country. That's Washakie, chief of the Shoshone Nation. He's been a friend to the white folk for a long while. He's even got a letter from the president himself, he has!"

The great chief of the Shoshone was just as impressive as all the things Jim had heard about him. He listened, entranced, as Levi explained the incursion of the Crow into Shoshone territory.

The Shoshone chief was impassive, but his eyes blazed. "Why would the yellow dogs who call themselves Crow come onto my land? Since the day I cut out the heart of the Crow chief on the butte, they have honored our hunting ground."

The reference piqued Jim's interest. "What's that about cutting someone's heart out?" he asked Levi.

Levi turned to explain, knowing Washakie would relish hearing the story repeated for the hundredth time. "There was a war brewin' between the Crow and the Shoshone a few years ago, over this huntin' ground. Instead of an all-out war, Washakie challenged the Crow's chief to a one-on-one combat. There's a butte up along Wind River with a big flat top. They agreed they would each climb that butte from their own side at sunup on the given day, and meet on top. Whichever one came back would be the winner, and the other tribe would leave."

"And Washakie won?"

Levi nodded. "It was pertnear sundown when he came back down off the butte. The Crow's heart was hangin' from his belt. He didn't say a word, from what I hear. The Crow rep in the Shoshone camp just jumped on his horse and rode off to tell the rest. They all pulled freight. They went up along the Yellowstone River in Montana Territory, where we found 'em, and they ain't bothered the Shoshone since."

"Wal, I'll be danged. What a way to fight a war! Dang shame the one I come outa wasn't fought that way, jist betwixt Lincoln an' Davis."

"Sometime you oughta ride up there just to look the spot over," Levi offered. "They call it 'Crow Heart Butte.' The thing that don't make any sense is why they'd come back, and risk a big war with the Shoshoni. It violates their word, and that just don't happen. Unless it was just that one small bunch, actin' on their own. But that don't make sense either."

Jim's head snapped up. "Uh, maybe somethin' I saw might shed some light on that," he said.

Levi and Washakie both came to attention as they waited expectantly. "Whilst I was a-tryin' to find that Indian camp, I almost rode into the same bunch o' Indians what kilt

Myra's man an' took her off. They met some white man what give 'em all rifles. They was a ways off, but it looked like either forty-four-forty or thirty-thirty carbines. Repeaters."

There was a long silence. It was Levi who finally broke it. "You mean somebody paid 'em to make that raid, and paid 'em with repeatin' rifles? Would they do that, Washakie?"

The imposing Indian considered it without expression. When he spoke it was with his usual voice of measured dignity. "It may be that among the Crow are some whose honor would not keep them from such a thing. A rifle that shoots many times would make each brave a warrior of great standing in his village. For such a prize, it could be they would do so, without the council of the Crows giving consent."

"Then the question would be who and why," Levi mused.

"You will find who has done this thing, Lightning Gun?"

Levi nodded. "I will find who has done this thing," he said softly. "I will do so because I am the friend of Washakie, but also because I believe it is my destiny to do so."

The chief nodded once and turned to his horse. Mounting, he rode away, with the band of Shoshoni following. As Levi had expected, they rode in pursuit of the fleeing Crow party. Jim frowned as he watched them go. "Lightning Gun?" he queried.

Levi shrugged. "It's just what they call me. They come to the ranch once in a while. Stubby, Myra's father, worked out a deal with them a long time ago. He gives 'em some cows for beef every year, and they make sure other Indians don't hassle us. I've stayed with 'em some. When you're accepted into their tribe, they give you a Shoshone name. That's just the one they hung on me."

"Lightning Gun?" Jim asked again.

Levi's eyes twinkled as he answered. "They just seem to be impressed with how my gun can get into my hand without them seein' me draw."

Jim seemed about to say something more, but Levi said, "Where's Myra?"

Jim cast frantic looks around, then pointed. A hundred yards away, Myra stood, rifle hanging loose in one hand, studying something on the ground.

The two men walked uneasily to where she stood. On the way they passed the bodies of the three Indians they had shot with their first fusillade. When they got close they realized she was standing over the body of yet another.

"Who's that?" Jim demanded.

Myra looked up at him, then back down at the lifeless body at her feet. "Many Thunders," she said.

"You got him?"

She took a deep, ragged breath. "When they started to leave, I stood up at the edge of the wallow. He spotted me, and turned back to see what I wanted. He was so sure of himself he probably thought I wanted him to take me back with him. When he stopped and started back, it gave me the chance I was waiting for. I didn't waste it."

She lifted her rifle. Shooting from the hip, she sent a projectile of hot lead into the unfeeling body of the man who had caused her such intense humiliation and misery. She levered another cartridge into the chamber and fired again. The force of the bullet's impact made the dead body twitch. She levered yet another cartridge into the barrel and fired again, then again and again until the hammer fell on an empty chamber. Then she turned wordlessly and walked back to where their horses still remained tied down.

"Remind me never to make that lady mad at me," Jim muttered.

As they released their horses and prepared to mount, Myra laid a hand on the body of her baby, still tied behind her saddle. Swiping at her cheek, she climbed into the saddle. Levi sighed heavily. "Myra, the boys from the ranch buried Tom in the graveyard back home. Do you want to bury Deborah beside him?"

Her eyes spilled onto her dusty cheeks as she nodded mutely.

The two men stepped up into their saddles. They rode away without a backward look at the dead warriors in the grass. Levi led the way. He made no comment about the fact that Jim and Myra rode together.

They rode together to the S R Bar ranch of Myra's parents. After a brief time of reunion, they led the horse bearing its macabre burden to the little cemetery on the hill behind the house. Some of the hands were just finishing the work of digging a small grave next to the fresh mound of dirt already there. Stubby recited the Twenty Third Psalm and said a few words with a choked voice. Then they lowered the blanket shrouded infant gently into the grave and replaced the dirt over her. Jim was more relieved than he would have liked to admit. The body was getting awfully ripe.

All the way home from their encounter with Washakie, Levi kept mulling over in his mind the revelation of the Indians' motive, or, more importantly, the motive of the one who purchased their incursion into Shoshone country with rifles. As he did, a resolution formed solidly in his mind.

"It may take a while," he thought, "but I'll find out who set that deal up. When I do, he's gonna think he's run into somethin' a whole lot worse than a mad Indian."

Chapter

Eleven

The air was electric. The patrons of the saloon crowded urgently away from the expected line of fire.

"Is this something official, or are you boys actin' on your own?" Levi asked softly.

The hulking sergeant glowered over the barrel of his army issue Colt revolver. "This is personal, little boy. Now get outa the way. That Johnny Reb tried to get my outfit killed, then he nearly killed me with a club. You ain't no part o' this."

"That 'Johnny Reb' whipped you good, soldier," Levi disagreed, "and he sure didn't use any club. He didn't need one. I was in that saloon when he did it. I watched it."

"Are you callin' me a liar?" the soldier snarled.

"You are a liar," Levi responded. "Even if I didn't call you that, you'd still be a liar. Oh, by the way, that Johnny Reb and me got the woman those Indians had kidnapped. We had to go rescue her ourselves, since your army didn't have anyone in it man enough for the job."

The soldier's eyes bugged from his engorged face. He sputtered for words. When he could find his voice, he bellowed at the four other soldiers with him, "Take 'em both! We're gonna hang these two sons o' …"

As he spoke the other soldiers lifted their rifles. Even as the sergeant was speaking, as the rifle barrels began to move, a 45 appeared as if by some impossible illusion in Levi's hand, spouting fire.

In a series of events too fast to comprehend, the sergeant took a sudden step backward. A hole appeared as if by magic in his chest. The 45 he was holding, trained on Levi, fell unfired from dying fingers. Soldiers lifted rifles too late, as each was driven back and down by shots so close together the sounds blurred into a single roar.

In an instant it was over. Levi and Jim stood side by side, watching for movement from five uniformed bodies on the saloon's floor.

"Lawsy!" Jim exclaimed. "I thought I was faster'n a greased rattlesnake. You done shot four o' them varmints afore I got one! Lawsy me! No wonder them Indians called you 'Lightnin' Gun'."

The doors of the saloon flew open and the sheriff burst in. As his eyes took in the scene, a deputy appeared at his elbow. Both had their guns drawn.

Slowly and deliberately, Levi holstered his gun. Jim followed suit, reluctantly.

"Sheriff," Levi said calmly, "these men are in uniform, but they were not acting on behalf of the army. Their intent was to hang this man over an old grudge, and me along with him. We shot in self-defense."

The sheriff looked a wordless question at the bartender. "Just like he says, Sheriff," the bartender agreed.

The sheriff looked around the room. The saloon's patrons were ungluing themselves from the outer walls. Several of them nodded their agreement.

The sheriff turned back to Levi. "You're that gunman that works for Rudabaugh."

Levi nodded. "I'm a cowboy, not a gunman. But I work for Rudabaugh. He raised me."

"Are you the one he sent to get his girl back from them Indians?"

Levi nodded again. "That's me. This here's Jim Keller. He's the one that followed 'em clear to Montana, and showed me where they were."

"What're you doin' in Laramie?"

"Tryin' to get a line on who paid the Crows in guns to get 'em to make that raid."

The sheriff's eyebrows shot up. "You think they was paid to do that?"

Levi nodded. "Jim saw a white man take 'em repeatin' rifles. That's the only way it makes sense."

The sheriff pondered it for a while. Then he turned to his deputy. "Slim, get the undertaker to take care of these bodies. I'll wire the army. Fort Kearney, you say?"
Jim and Levi nodded in unison.

"You boys had best come with me till we find out what the army says."

It was three hours later when they walked out of the telegraph office. "I don't know for the life of me why folks can't let the war be over," the sheriff complained. "Imagine, them goin' AWOL and trailing you clear down here, 'cause they was still sore over the war."

"It'll take a lot more years than that for the wounds to heal," Jim observed. "It'll likely take generations."

"So what're you boys plannin' next?"

Levi and Jim looked at each other. It was Levi who answered. "I 'spect Jim oughta be headin' back to the S R Bar. Myra sorta seems to want him pretty close, and she's havin' trouble fightin' off the melancholy yet. I think I'll keep nosin' around. Sooner or later, I'll figure out who hates Stubby, or his daughter, or the man she was married to, enough to hire Indians to kill 'em."

Levi rode into Kaycee alone nearly a month later. He had nothing whatever to show for a month in the saddle. Countless conversations in bunkhouses, homestead shacks, ranch houses and saloons had disclosed exactly nothing.

Even so, he found himself enjoying the challenge. It was a side to his nature he had never had occasion to discover before. He felt a constant tingling excitement at the pursuit of information he needed. He felt that excitement surge each time some chance conversation promised a clue to the consuming question that kept him moving always to one more town, one more ranch, one more saloon.

He had developed a pattern as he probed for a motive behind the Indian raid. Each town he entered, he would begin with the office of the sheriff or the town marshal. He would identify himself, explain his mission, and ask for any information the law officer might have. Then he would move on to the saloon, the hotel lobby, the livery barn, the church, anywhere people gathered to gossip. He especially enjoyed the churches. There he heard erudite sermons that would have shamed those delivered in the great cathedrals of the east or Europe from humble and nearly destitute preachers. There he also learned the intimate heartbeat of the area's citizenry as they visited in the churchyard after the services. It was not only a vital refreshment for his own faith. It was just as vital a source of information.

It was a lonesome country. Spaces were great and people were spread thinly. Any place of gathering became a place of sharing information and excitement. Cowboys, especially, were a lonesome breed. Anything that moved on the range they noted, and it became a topic of conversation and speculation in future gatherings.

That's the way reputations grew as well. By now, every place Levi went, the story of the gunfight in the Laramie saloon had already preceded him. The last thing in the world he wanted was the reputation of a gunman, but it hounded him relentlessly.

He had known he was different from most men since before he was a man. He had been feared and hated almost as much as respected and admired. He was far too strong. He was much too quick. He was far, far too good as a fighter. To be different is always a difficult burden to bear, even when different means better than anyone else. He could have used his phenomenal physical abilities to take anything he wanted, but he would not. He held himself to such a rigid moral code he would not use his prowess except in defense of himself or someone else. People hated and feared him anyway. He was different.

He learned how strongly that difference would affect his life while he was still in the Sixth Reader at school. When he was forced to defend himself against a trio of bullies, he whipped all three of them easily and thoroughly. Instead of being a hero to his girl friend, he suddenly became onerous to her. Sarah Ferguson thought he was the finest boy she had ever known, until that day. After that day, she wouldn't even speak to him. It was the sudden end of his first and last romance.

It was being different that made his life since that day so lonely. He was alone, even in the house of the family who raised him. In the bunkhouse he was just as alone, but it didn't feel so wrong to be alone there, so that's where he lived. It actually felt good to Levi to be drifting around the country alone, seeking clues to explain Myra's abduction and the murders of her husband and subsequent murder of her baby. A lone drifter is supposed to be alone, without friends, without family. Now his being different was being made even greater by a reputation he neither wanted nor knew how to prevent.

It was that reputation that prompted the town marshal of Kaycee to offer him a warning. "Monte West is in town."

Levi looked blankly at the marshal. "Monte West?"

"You've never heard of him?"

Levi shook his head. The marshal explained. "He's supposed to be some sort of fast gun. I got no idea whether he is, or just thinks he is. He's gonna get himself killed either way, sooner or later. He spends his time at the saloon, braggin' about how fast he is."

"Why should that concern me? Do you think he might be involved in the Indian raid?"

"Nope. Not likely. It's just that he thinks he's a fast gun, so he'll most likely need to find out if he's faster'n you are."

This was a new problem to deal with. He was totally uncomfortable with the reputation that had begun to dog him. Now it made a tight knot in his stomach. Was he likely to have to kill someone, just because that someone wanted a reputation? He had heard of such a thing happening, but he had only half believed it, thinking it mostly fodder for the dime novels. At any rate, the whole idea had always been remote. As soon as he walked into the saloon it ceased to be remote.

He hadn't made it from the front door to the bar when the buzz of conversation sputtered to a halt clear through the room. The last two steps to that bar were made in a silence so intense he could hear his boots rustle the sawdust on the floor. He had no idea who had identified him, but it was obvious someone had.

In a volume exaggerated by the hush in the air, a young voice accosted him. "Is that true? Are you the Levi Hill?"

Levi looked into the face of the challenger and felt the blood drain from his face. He was just a kid! The boy facing him couldn't have been more than seventeen or eighteen years old. His lip showed a pitiful attempt at a moustache he wasn't old enough to grow yet. His eyes sparkled with excitement. His hand hovered over the butt of a Colt .44. It was holstered low, tied down.

The boy himself was comically overdressed. His hat was the highest crown and broadest brim that a haberdasher might have made. His neckerchief was bright red silk. He wore chaps with silver conches that showed not a single mark or scar of brush or a rope having dragged across them. He wore well-polished spurs, even here in the saloon. His silk shirt was partially covered by a vest of white leather. He looked like a drawing from one of those dime novels.

Levi thought he was going to be sick. The thought of having to kill a misguided kid nauseated him. Even so, he knew some of the west's most cold-blooded killers had appeared just that young, fresh, and out of place.

He turned back to the bar, choosing to ignore the challenge. He addressed the bartender. "I'd like a beer."

The bartender set a beer on the bar and took his nickel, looking worried. He moved quickly to the other end of the bar. The young man stood just at Levi's left. His face reddened with Levi's rebuff. "Don't try to ignore me!" he said, too loudly. "I'm your worst bad dream, because I'm the fastest man with a gun you'll ever face. I'm calling you out, if you aren't a coward."

Levi looked him slowly up and down, then turned back to the bar. "Go home and get some decent clothes on and get a job," he growled.

The young boy's face took on yet a deeper shade of red. He hissed, "You'll die for that, whether you're too yellow to draw your gun or not!"

As the youth grabbed for his gun, Levi swung the mug of beer with his left hand. It crashed against the would-be gunman's left temple with a resounding "thunk," flinging beer across half the room. He sprawled to the floor and lay without moving, his gun still in its holster.

The silence of the saloon erupted into excited chatter. A rancher approached Levi. "That was downright purty," he appreciated. "I thought sure you was goin' to have to kill that boy, just for bein' so drunk and so dumb."

Levi shook his head sadly. The rancher continued, "I'd be proud to buy you a beer to replace the one you spilled." The conversation slowly returned to normal in the room. Levi slipped the gun from the holster of the unconscious challenger and gave it to the bartender. "Give it back to him when he sobers up," he said.

It was soon obvious he was going to learn nothing from this stop. He suddenly felt an overwhelming urgency to get out of town, to head for the mountains, to be alone. The idea of being alone by himself didn't sound nearly as lonely as the sense of being alone here, in the middle of a saloon filled with people.

He thanked the friendly rancher for the beer and headed out the door, leaving the beer untouched on the bar. He had retrieved his horse from the livery barn and was just ready to mount up, when a cold voice froze him in his tracks.

"That was awful, how you shamed that kid," the voice said. Levi turned slowly. The man who stood in the street facing him was no older than the one now on the floor of the saloon. That was the end of the similarity.

The shine in the eyes of this young man was cold and hard. There was an eager look of anticipation on his face that made him look like he was licking his lips even when he wasn't. His face was pale with tense excitement. His hand hung in a deceptively relaxed appearance, inches from his gun.

It was the perfect match between the ice in the voice and in the eyes that spun Levi's senses into a heightened sense of alert. "Better shamed than dead. Who are you?" he asked, trying to sound casual.

"Don't matter," the other dismissed the question. "I just gotta know if you're faster'n me."

"What difference does it make?" Levi protested.

The ice in the other's eyes flashed cold fire. "It matters to me. I'm gonna toss this rock over on to the sidewalk. When it hits the board, I'm gonna draw my gun and kill you. If you're fast enough, you can maybe at least get your gun outa the holster afore you're dead."

Levi started to protest, but there was no hesitation in the man at all. He casually tossed the stone in his hand toward the board sidewalk.

Levi wasn't listening. He was watching the man in front of him. The stone hadn't hit yet when something in that man triggered his reflexes. His gun leaped into his hand and roared, even as his senses recorded the other man was, in fact, drawing before the signal. The roar of his gun drowned out whatever sound the stone made.

A look of stunned disbelief crossed the pinched face of the gunman. It was replaced by pain that passed momentarily across it, then the blankness of death overwhelmed both as his face touched the dust of the street.

Excited voices and the stamping of feet spilled from the saloon. There was a circle of gawkers gathered in a matter of seconds. Questions spilled over each other until the town marshal stepped through the circle of morbid curiosity. "What happened here?" he demanded.

Levi holstered his gun with a sigh. "This man braced me. He said he'd kill me whether I drew on him or not. Then he went for his gun. He wasn't fast enough."

The marshal's eyes swept over the dead man, his gun still unfired in his hand. He looked around the circle of faces. "Anyone see it?"

There were several heartbeats of silence, then the rancher who had bought Levi's replacement beer spoke up. "I didn't see it, but I'd sure believe him. That kid that calls himself Monte West tried to make him draw in the saloon. Hill knocked him out so he wouldn't have to kill him. If he says this man gave him no choice, I'd sure believe him."

A murmur of voices assented. The marshal nodded. "I see no reason to believe otherwise. Hill, I'd be obliged if you'd get outa town, though. Your reputation draws trouble like dead meat draws flies."

"That ain't my choice," Levi protested.

The marshal nodded understandingly, but firmly. "I know

that. But I gotta run a half-way peaceable town. I'd give you a word of advice, though."

"What's that?"

"Try lawin'. The only thing that'll keep your reputation from drawin' every would-be gunman in Wyoming, is for you to wear a badge. There's somethin' about the badge that sorta changes that. Get yourself a job lawin' as a marshal, or workin' for that Pinkerton outfit, or somethin' like that. Use your reputation to get your job done, 'stead o' lettin' it chase you all over the country."

The words of advice formed a cradle in which Levi rocked his despondency and loneliness as he rode out of town.

Chapter Twelve

Eyes bored into the back of Levi's head as he rode out of Kaycee. The skin on his neck tingled. He fought the urge to lie low onto his horse's neck and spur him into a dead run. He had never had the experience of being a target just because he was fast with a gun. He suddenly felt the presence of hidden assailants on all sides.

As he left the buildings of the main street, heading west, the sensation of imminent danger began to abate. Houses set well back from the dust of the road seemed to pose no threat. He rode past the schoolhouse, almost smiling at the children playing in the school yard.

Then he spotted a lone boy, standing off to the side of a playground game in progress. His face bore no expression. He just stood there, watching the others play. He was not invited to join. He did not ask. Memories of being that "outsider" drew Levi's lips into a pale thin line.

Just past the school the road dipped across a small dry gully. As his horse climbed the far side, movement from the corner of his eye brought him whirling in the saddle. His gun leaped into hand, fully cocked.

He lowered the hammer and replaced it in the holster, frowning. Hesitating only a moment, he turned his horse back into the gully.

Riding up the bottom of the narrow gulch, he was within a few feet of a group of schoolboys before they saw him. Two boys were holding a third. A fourth boy was intent on beating the one held by his two buddies. He was hampered only by the feet of the one held captive.

The two holding his arms were too strong for him to wrest free, but they could not haul him to the ground, and could not keep him from using his feet. Each time the one intent on delivering the beating approached, a well-placed foot either sent him sprawling or doubled him in pain.

Even so, Levi knew it was just a matter of time until the greater numbers would bear the lad's courage to the ground. There was no doubt he would be severely beaten when that happened.

"You boys havin' fun?" he asked softly.

The effect was spectacular. The two boys holding the other's arms dropped them like they were stung, and leaped away from him. They stood stock still, stunned by the unexpected intrusion that had caught their cowardly actions red-handed. The one who had been trying to administer the beating whirled to look at Levi for an instant, then back at his suddenly released victim. The instant's hesitation was all the other boy needed.

That boy didn't hesitate. In a lunge he was on top of his nemesis, fists flying. It was no match. Levi stared at the two who had released their victim, daring them with his eyes to try to interfere. They made no such effort.

When the would-be victim had administered as much of a beating as Levi thought appropriate, he stopped it. "That's enough," he barked.

The boy stopped, fist poised. He looked over his shoulder at Levi, then looked again at the recipient of his rage. The bigger boy's nose was bleeding. A cut over one eye bled profusely. His lips were rapidly swelling out of proportion. Bruises covered his cheeks.

The smaller boy nodded with apparent satisfaction and stepped back. "You gonna let me whip them too?" he asked, nodding toward the two who had attempted to hold him down.

Levi looked at him contemplatively. "What's this all about?"

"I whipped Jed the other day, in a fair fight. He called me out again today. He said it'd just be the two of us, over here in the gully at recess. But when I got here, they grabbed me, to hold me for 'im."

Levi addressed the other two obviously frightened boys. "Why?"

They both swallowed hard, then swallowed again. The redheaded one finally found his tongue. "Cuz Jed said he'd whip me if I didn't help."

"Did that make it right?" Levi asked softly.

Neither boy answered. He let the silence hang heavily for a long moment before he spoke again.

"Let me tell you something. You boys lost something today. You might be able to get it back again, if you're big enough. You lost a big chunk of your manhood. You let yourselves be pushed into doing something you knew was wrong. If you'd taken a whipping from Jed, all you'd have lost would have been a little skin. When you let him bully you into doing what you didn't want to do, you lost your pride. The skin would've grown back. Bruises heal. Shame doesn't heal that easily. For the rest of your lives you'll remember how you let yourselves be used by a bully."

"What in the world is going on here?"

Levi jumped as hard as the boys at the imperious voice. The school teacher stood on the rim of the gully, hands on hips. All four boys cringed. Levi fought the urge to grin.

He touched his hat brim. "Ma'am. You'd be the school-marm?"

"I am the school teacher. I seem to be missing four of my students following recess. Matthew, are you fighting again?"

"Now just a minute, Ma'am," Levi broke in. "I sorta rode onto this deal, and I' 'spect you'd oughta know how it is. These two was a-holdin that one, so that one over there could work him over. He would've, too, if I hadn't happened by."

"Who are you?"

"The name's Levi Hill, Ma'am. I'm just passin' through."

Her lips compressed even tighter. Half-moon creases formed at the corners of her mouth. It was obvious she had heard the name, and despised it before she had even met him. "You're a fine one to be talking to schoolboys! And did you countenance this beating of Jedediah?"

"Seemed sorta fair," Levi said, squirming at his own defensiveness. His ears burned fiercely.

"Then you are certainly no better and no more mature than any of them. You will oblige me by removing your presence and your unsavory influence from the vicinity of my school. Get along now! Go!"

Levi fought a rising tide of anger that collided with the intimidation he felt. For an instant a desire surged within him to force this imperious woman to back down in front of her students. The desire rose as an opportunity for revenge against every embarrassment and humiliation by every teacher he had as a child. Just as quickly the desire was replaced by the conviction that he could not do so.
He looked at the boy he had rescued. "You'll be ok?"
The boy nodded mutely. He looked at the two who had been bullied into helping commit the atrocity. "You boys remember what I told you."

With that he lifted the reins and turned his horse away. He resisted the urge to look over his shoulder at the sounds of four pairs of feet scrambling up the side of the gully and heading toward the schoolhouse on a dead run. It was not purely a controlling of curiosity. It was just as much a determination that the school teacher not see the redness of his face. Was this the way the rest of his life was to be?

"Shore do make a feller seem small, don't they?"

Levi jumped at the voice, cursing himself for not even seeing the horseman who had fallen in beside him on the road.

"Jim!" he said, recognizing his friend almost as soon as he jumped. "I thought you were down on the S R Bar."

"Sorta got curious," Keller explained. "Thought maybe I'd best see if'n I could keep you outa trouble. Never thought it'd be some schoolmarm you was in trouble with, though."

Levi chuckled in spite of himself. "What is it about a school teacher that makes a grown man feel like a kid?"

"Rememberin' too many of 'em with a willow switch," Jim replied dryly. "My hind-side still smarts every time I see a school house, an' I only got through the Third Reader."

Levi chose to ignore the remark and changed the subject. "How'd you find me?"

"Foller'd the stories. You're gettin' to be a reg'lar legend!"

Levi sighed heavily. "Not my idea. I never heard of anything like it. Everywhere I go, all anybody can talk about is how many people I've killed, and how fast I am. I've heard more stories about myself than I have about Pecos Bill and Paul Bunyan put together, and none of 'em even close to bein' true."

"What've you found?"

"Nothing. I haven't got one single thing. I stayed around close to Laramie for a while, then started ranging farther north, but I've found nothing."

"You still think it was revenge o' some sort?"

"Can't figure anything else that makes sense. It had to

be somebody that knew the Indians. He had to know the Crow would like a chance to put one over on Washakie and the Shoshoni if they could. He had to know how bad they wanted repeatin' rifles. He had to know where to find 'em. And it had to be directed straight at Tom and Myra. The raiding party kept their heads down and didn't touch anybody until after they hit their homestead. Then they raided everything they could on the way home."

"So it had to be somebody with a reason that involved Tom'n Myra," Jim agreed.

They continued to rehash all the things they had said to each other a dozen times before as they rode toward the Big Horn Mountains, west from Kaycee.

It was enough just to be away from towns and people for the first three days. Levi began to relax again. The stream they rode along laughed over rocks and gravel with a crystal voice. Trout flashed in the clear riffles. He caught a couple of them that evening, and they cooked them over a small fire while they talked the sun down behind the mountains. During the night they heard thunder over the mountains, but it did not rain.

Levi rose at first light to catch some fish for breakfast. They rode out an hour later. By noon they had entered a broad valley, just as pristine and beautiful as the one they had left. Levi rode on ahead when Jim stopped to pick a hatful of raspberries to eat as he rode. He was frowning at the creek rushing through that valley when Jim joined him. "What kinda burr's under your saddle this mornin'?"

"Look at the crick."

"Wal, I'll be jiggered. It's muddier'n the Mizzouri."

"I've never seen a crick turn that muddy in the mountains. Musta rained awful hard up higher last night."

"It does that every other day or so, but I never saw it make a crick that muddy."

"Let's follow it. Maybe we can see why."

Several miles up along the muddy stream they came into yet another beautiful high valley. It stretched for miles, with patches of aspen and evergreen timber. Wild flowers decorated the meadows with splashes of brilliant colors. Lush grass brushed their horses' bellies as they walked.

"If heaven's any purtier'n this, it's enough to make you wanta be good," Jim breathed.

Levi nodded, breathing in the scene as though he could inhale its beauty and serenity. Against the background of pristine beauty, the stream, rushing brown and dirty, looked even more repugnant.

"Let's see what we can find," Levi growled.

It was late that afternoon when they began to find the reasons. The beaver dams that fill every high mountain valley were all ripped open. They appeared to have been blown apart with dynamite.

The beaver huts, normally more than half below the surface of the water, had been exposed and ripped open. The rains, unchecked by the dams' slowing and cleansing influence, eroded land into muddy sludge that fouled the waters. They finally came to the remains of a crude cabin that had been hastily thrown together. Trash was strewn everywhere.

Bones littered the area.

Through tight lips, Levi breathed a single word. "Foster!"

"Who's Foster?" Jim asked. A deadly softness cushioned the edges of his words.

"He's a trapper. Stubby had me run him off a couple or three years ago. He doesn't trap an area. He just wipes it out. Kills everything he can't catch. He plumb ruins everything he touches. Stubby don't mind trappers. Most of 'em just trap off the excess and move on. They help keep things in balance. Guys like Foster just wreck it."

"Rape."

"What?"

"It's rape," Jim said again. "The land's like a fine and noble lady. You can love her and take care of her, and she'll love you back. Or you can rape her. Use her and destroy her, then throw her away."

"Regular philosopher, ain't you?"

Jim didn't smile. "A man like that oughta be gut-shot, then left to die slow and painful like the land he's ruined."

Levi nodded. "Stubby pertnear did when he saw what he was doin' up in the mountains above the S R Bar. He told Foster that's exactly what he'd do if he ever saw him again."

"Left without a fight though, huh?"

Levi didn't answer for several heartbeats. Then he said, "He left."

Jim did not press for details.

Levi looked a full circle at the rotting scene of destruction, wondering how many years it would take the land to heal itself. Then a new thought hit him.

"Damn!"

Jim looked up in surprise. "What bit you?"

"My stupidity," Levi said angrily. "I've been runnin' all over the country tryin' to find somethin', and it was in my head all the time."

Jim only looked confused. "You lost me."

"We've been lookin' for somebody who knows Indians, knows Stubby and his family, knows the country, and has some reason to risk his own hide to hurt Stubby and his family. In other words, it's gotta be some sort of revenge. When Stubby had me run Foster off, Foster told him he'd rue the day he'd done that. He told him he'd better sleep real light and keep his kids locked up for the rest of his life, 'cause Merton Foster wasn't someone to have for an enemy."

"So you think he's the one?"

"I can't think of a better candidate."

They sat in silence for a long while, as the pieces of the puzzle fell into place in Levi's mind. "How you gonna find out for sure?" Jim asked finally.

"That's what I'm workin' on," Levi responded. "The key has to be the guns. If we can find out he's the one that bought a dozen or so repeating rifles, we'll have our man for sure."

"That'd take a fair chunk o' money."

"Or a lot of furs. Let's go back to Kaycee. That's the closest place to here that trades furs. This is the place he trapped last winter, it looks like. If we can find the fur trader he dealt with, maybe we can get a lead."

They made it back to Kaycee in two days. Levi insisted they stop at the marshal's office as soon as they hit town. The marshal was less than ecstatic to see Levi. "You cause more trouble in one day than I can settle down in a week," he grumbled. "I even had the school teacher in here complainin' about you! Then when I finally get things settled down, you show up again."

"Who's the fur dealer in town?" Levi asked, ignoring the marshal's tale of woe.

"Gus Trevor. His outfit's over by the crick on the east end o' town. Just outa smellin' range of most houses, 'cept when the wind's wrong. Why?"

Levi briefly apprised him of their discovery and their suspicions. "Now that'd be something I'd be plumb awful interested in," the marshal said, leaning forward in his chair. "Selling guns or whiskey either one to the Indians will get you hung about as quick as horse stealin' around here. I'll come with you."

The fur trader's place was identifiable by the smell even before they could see it. It may have been that smell that caused Levi to dislike the man even before he met him. It was obvious from their expressions that his companions shared the feeling.

The appearance of the trader did nothing to improve their attitude. He was a small, greasy man who squinted through ill-fitting glasses. He emanated the same smell as his establishment.

No furs were evident, as it was summer, but their presence was well attested by the essence that lingered.

"Mert Foster sell hides to you?" the marshal asked bluntly without preamble.

The mousy trader squinted at the three in turn before answering. Levi had the feeling he was scouting the edges of the room for a hole to dart into, should he need to do so. "Some," he answered in a nasal whine. "Why?"

The marshal ignored the question. "Does he trade 'em for anything besides money?"

"What do you mean?"

"Did he trade you his furs, or just sell 'em to you outright?"

"Well now, that's pryin' into a man's business, Marshal. You got no call to pry into how I run my business. I ain't done nothin' illegal."

"Just answer the question," the marshal growled, "or I'll go back to my office and let these two boys ask you the questions their way. This here's Levi Hill."

Silence became suddenly deafening. The trader's nervousness escalated to agitation. "Now listen, you got no call to turn no gunman loose on me. I ain't done nothin' wrong.

If a trapper wants to trade his furs for guns 'stead o' cash, that's his business."

"Who said anything about guns?" Levi asked softly. Jim had moved around behind the trader. He scuffed his feet on the floor to make his presence there obvious. The trader's eyes whipped around the circle of the three who now had him hemmed in on all sides.

"Didn't you say 'guns'?" he squeaked. "I thought sure you said somethin' about guns. I'm just a trader. I just trade for furs. If you want to know anything about what Foster wanted them guns for, you'll have to ask him. I don't ask no questions. I don't want no trouble. Just go away an' leave me alone!"

"How many guns?" Levi demanded, allowing a hard edge to his voice.

The trader's Adam's apple bobbed uncontrollably. His eyes darted around the circle of his inquisitors. In a voice reminding Levi even more of a mouse he squeaked, "Twelve. A dozen. Winchester. Forty-four-forties. I got 'em from Blumenthal. I got no idea what he wanted with 'em. He said he had a market for 'em. If he can sell 'em an' make money, that's his business, not mine."

Levi looked at the shriveled trader a moment longer. A glance at his companions saw their faces mirroring his own revulsion. Wordlessly he wheeled and walked out. The other two followed close behind.

Chapter Thirteen

There was no warning. There was that same feeling, that had become a familiar precursor of danger, but that's all it was. The feeling was there when he and Jim rolled out of their bedrolls that morning. It was there as a prickly sensation along the back of his neck. It was there as an extra tightness in his stomach. It was there as some vague premonition of impending threat. It just wasn't definable. It wasn't clear. It lacked the substance necessary to constitute a warning.

They were two weeks out of Kaycee. At least they knew who they were looking for now. The pieces of the puzzle had finally fallen together. There was enough evidence to convince Levi that Merton Foster had used repeating rifles to entice the Crow to invade Shoshone land, raid the homestead of Stubby Rudabaugh's daughter and her husband, and kill them. Levi thought the idea of carrying off the woman and her baby as captives had been a spur of the moment idea of Many Thunders, not part of the agreement. He had simply been too entranced by her red hair and her courage. That would explain the white man's anger when he delivered the rifles in payment.

The problem now was to find Foster. It was unlikely that

he would move too far. His trap line required too much paraphernalia to move everything farther than necessary. He had to move, though. In one trapping season he totally destroyed the area in which he trapped. They could find and identify every valley he had trapped along the eastern range of the Big Horn Mountains. It would take years, decades even, for the land to recover from the wanton destruction he wreaked on it in one trapping season.

"It'll be a fine thing for the land, just to get rid of this mangy hog lover," Jim had observed a couple of days ago. Levi agreed, inwardly as well as outwardly. He felt an intense revulsion at the man's total disregard for everything except his own profit. It was the same revulsion he felt against the buffalo hunters. The destruction they left behind was the same.

They could tell, from the extent of the recovery in each of the valleys he had trapped, what general direction Foster was working. They were confident they were getting closer to finding him.

It was still summer, but drawing toward autumn. That meant he should be getting pretty well entrenched somewhere. He needed to be well in place by trapping season, when the pelts became prime and valuable with their winter density. They should be able to find him.

Maybe it was the expectation of finding him soon that caused that uneasy feeling Levi got up with today. Maybe his instincts knew they were getting close. Maybe he just wanted it to end.

They had crossed the watershed two days ago. He was fairly sure the land they rode now drained to the Wind River. That meant Foster would either have to haul his furs across the pass in the spring, or find a new fur trader. Either one would pose no real problem.

By mid-morning they began to see signs of a white man's passing. More than that, the signs matched Foster's nature. Two camp fires had been left to burn themselves out. At each site, Levi quickly noted places where the occupant of the camp site had relieved himself almost within reach of the fire. "Too lazy to walk into the bushes," he muttered to himself. "He'd rather smell himself all night than take an extra six steps."

The feeling that had wakened him that morning persisted. He found himself loosening his rifle in its saddle scabbard twice. Shortly after their discovery of the second camp site, he had unhooked the keeper strap from his .45, readying it for quick access. He was just nervous.

Even so, it caught him totally by surprise. He and Jim were riding side by side up a broad valley. A quarter of a mile to their right, they could hear the chuckling of a nice sized stream. Small clumps of timber dotted the valley. It was another of those picturesque mountain valleys that must have been God's pride and joy in creation.

The late summer wild flowers dipped and nodded in the soft breeze. A huge bull moose watched their passing with bored disinterest, then resumed his shambling walk toward some unseen swampy area to feed. It was so quiet Levi could hear the occasional buzz of a bee.

The first hint of trouble was the harsh grunt from Jim, riding three feet to his right. As he whirled to see why his companion made such a strange noise, the unmistakable roar of a .50 Sharps reached his ears. From the grove of aspen ahead of them he caught a glimpse of gun-smoke as the breeze caught it away.

Levi grabbed his carbine from the saddle scabbard as he dived headlong for the tall grass. He heard, rather than saw, Jim hit the ground ten feet to his right. Moving quickly he crawled to his fallen comrade. "How bad you hit?" he whispered as he approached.

"Ain't shore yet," Jim grated. "Did you see where that varmint is?"

"That grove of aspen. You gonna make it a while?"

"Go get the yellow-bellied son-of-a-buck. I'll be fine."

Levi looked hard at his companion. A spreading red stain on the left side of his abdomen left no doubt where he had been hit. It was far enough to the left it just might have missed vital organs. Even so, he would need attention, and quickly, if he were to survive.

In the grove of aspen was a man he had already devoted the whole summer to finding and stopping. He had a duty to his employer, as well as to his own concept of justice, to not let him escape. Nothing held Levi in as firm a grip as his sense of duty. Now, however, he felt a duty in two conflicting and demanding directions.

"He likely high-tailed it already," he muttered. "I best check it out, though. Keep your gun ready and your head down."

"I didn't survive Bull Run bein' dumb," Jim returned sourly.

Levi crawled away quickly. Moving carefully to move no more grass than necessary, he crawled toward a shallow draw he had noticed to his left. He hadn't even been aware of noticing it, until he needed to know the lay of the land. Then it was there, as it was with most of the true western men he knew. Watching the land, the sky, the horizon, was a thing that was so basic to survival those who did survive did it without even noticing that they were doing so.

He reached the depression without incident. With its greater cover, he raised to a crouch and followed it at a run for four hundred yards. Then he risked a careful peek over the edge of the shallow defile to assess his position.

He was within a hundred yards of the edge of the aspen trees. There were frequent clumps of brush and rock out-croppings between himself and the timber. Using them as cover, he flitted across short open spaces, never exposing himself for more than a couple seconds at a time.

His approach was either unnoticed or ignored. It drew no response.

Reaching the fringe of the aspen grove, he crouched behind a wild plum bush and listened intently. There was no sound that was out of place in the still meadow. He could see Jim's horse and his own standing where they had stopped, reins dragging the ground.

After listening for several minutes, Levi began to circle away from the spot the shot had come from. If his approach had been noted, there would certainly be an ambush set up on a direct route to that spot. Accordingly, he circled widely, watching the ground for any sign of recent passage.

He found it almost at once. He could see clear sign of a man walking in the direction of the focus of his hunt. A second set of sign betrayed a hasty retreat from the site.Thoughtfully and carefully, he chose to follow the tracks. He did so from as far to the side as he could maintain the trail, to minimize the chance of ambush.

As the tracks got farther from the point of the shot being fired, they showed signs of increasing haste. Levi stood still to study them.

"Moccasins, and travelin' on foot," he muttered. "He's on the run now. He'll likely lay up and wait somewhere, to see if he's bein' followed. Then he'll shoot from ambush again." He chewed on his lip. He wanted to follow the trail at once. He knew he was expert enough at tracking to follow as fast as the trapper could run. He also knew the man would not expect pursuit that quickly or that fast.

He also knew his friend was wounded. He might survive until Levi could track down the trapper, and either kill him or capture him. Then again, he might not.

He sighed heavily. With an instinctive caution, he retraced the trapper's tracks to the point from which he had fired the shot. He quickly found the spent casing, confirming it was, in fact, a .50 caliber weapon. He dropped the casing in his pocket and returned quickly to his downed companion. "It's me, Jim," he said as he approached where he had left his friend.

His first glimpse of his friend confirmed his concern. Jim's face was twisted with pain. He was so pale his lips had no color at all. He had removed his shirt and wadded his neckerchief into the bullet wound in an effort to staunch the bleeding. It had been only partially successful.

Levi looked the wound over carefully. "The bullet went clear through," he said. "You're bleedin' out the back too."

He took off his own neckerchief and wadded it into the bullet's exit hole. Then he took Jim's shirt and folded it into a narrow band. Wrapping it around him, he tied it as tightly as he could, binding both waddings into place. Then he sat back on his heels to consider the matter.

"How bad is it?" Jim asked, sounding almost breathless.

"It ain't as bad as it might be," Levi said. "I didn't see or smell any sign your guts is busted. If he didn't bust a gut, you'll be okay, if we can get you somewhere you'll be cared for. You ain't gonna ride, though.

"Yeah, well I don't reckon the general's ambulance wagon is fixin' to drop by today, though," Jim responded.

Levi didn't answer for a long while. Finally he said, "Well, then, I guess we'll just have to holler at the general and tell 'im to."

Walking back to the aspen grove, Levi gathered as big an armload of sticks as he could carry. Returning to his companion, he found a rocky spot of ground. Dropping the load of kindling, he cleared the grass from a space of the rocky ground. Then he arranged the wood and started a fire. While the fire burned, he went to his horse and got his bedroll. He removed a blanket, dropping it close to the fire. He got his canteen and offered Jim a drink. He accepted it greedily.

He fed wood onto the fire for half an hour, building up a large pile of red hot coals. Then he started pulling handfuls of green grass. When he had a fair-sized pile of grass beside the fire, he squatted beside it. He moved the blanket up close beside him.

He dropped a double handful of the grass onto the fire. Immediately it began to send up a spire of white smoke. He nodded with satisfaction as he saw the smoke ascend almost vertically until it was more than a hundred feet above the ground.

He picked up the blanket. With a sweeping motion, he covered the fire. The blanket put an effective lid on the smoke for a few seconds. When the smoke began to spill out from around the edges of the blanket, Levi whipped it aside, allowing a puff of smoke to ascend. Then he quickly covered the fire again.

For several minutes he continued to send a series of puffs of smoke into the sky. Several short puffs were followed by a long puff, sometimes two long puffs in a row. Then he kicked the grass from the coals, stamping out each smoldering clump quickly and carefully.

He took the canteen to Jim again, offering him another drink. He again drank greedily.

As though he hadn't a care in the world, Levi unsaddled both horses. He hobbled their front feet to keep them from wandering too far, and let them go. He set up a camp site beside his wounded friend. He kindled the coals into another small, smokeless fire and started coffee.

Every few minutes Levi rose to the limit of his height and scanned the distance in all directions. Almost thirty minutes after he had stamped out the signal fire, he caught a glimpse of smoke far to the west. Staring intently, he made out several distinct puffs of smoke. He smiled.

"Well, my friend," he said, speaking aloud for the first time in a while, "I think the general's on the way."

Jim did not answer. Consciousness had slipped away. Having occasion to send a smoke signal caused Levi to relive a very difficult summer. Because of the deaths of his family at the hands of Indians, he had borne a pathological hatred of the entire race. When he was twelve, Stubby Rudabaugh sent him to live with the Shoshone for a year.

He had tried to explain the differences between the different tribes of Indians to Levi for several years. The Shoshone were among those the rancher counted as friends. To Levi, they were all just Indians.

He had protested vigorously when sent away with them, but it had taught him what he needed to learn. The Indians were people. There were good, and there were bad among them. There were the energetic and ambitious, and there were the lazy. There were the brave and the cowardly, the honest and the sneak thieves.

He had never learned so much, so quickly, in his life. Among the Indians his physical prowess was marveled at and deeply appreciated, even at twelve years of age. They taught him a great deal of hunting, tracking, stalking, and living from the fruits of the land. They taught him to make moccasins, tan hides, and many other things. He had spent four summers with them since, by his own choice, and had many strong friendships there.

He wondered now, as he waited, whether the response to his signal would include any whom he knew.

Chapter Fourteen

The sun cast long shadows down the side of the mountain. It made the shadows of the four Indians stretch into distorted patterns of savagery. In spite of his extreme weakness, Jim was obviously nervous. Levi, however, squatted beside his friend, waiting impassively for the Indians to approach.

After he had sent the smoke signals, Levi had eaten and rolled into his blankets. Every hour through the night he had risen to check his friend and give him water. Jim had offered no word of complaint, nor made any sound, but he had slept little. The fever had come with the morning sun. The Indians rode around them and approached with the sun at their back. Levi smiled quietly. If he were not secure in their friendship, he wouldn't ever have allowed them to position themselves between him and the sun. But these were Shoshoni. He had signaled for them. He needed their help.

The Indians dismounted. Three stood by their horses as the fourth approached. "I am Yellow Spotted Pony. You are the Gun of Lightning?"

Levi chose to answer in the Shoshone language instead of English. He noticed the slight surprise that crossed the Indian's face before he masked it. "I am Lightning Gun. I am honored to meet Yellow Spotted Pony. My friend Washakie has spoken of you. You are a great warrior. It is an honor to a white man to have friends among the Shoshone."

Yellow Spotted Pony replied in his own, more familiar and comfortable tongue. "You have sent the smoke that asks for a medicine man."

From there their conversation was a mixture of English and Shoshone. "My friend has been shot. I cannot take him to the white doctor. I wish for him to be taken to the town of Kaycee."

"It is a long way."

"It is a long way," Levi responded. "If I try to take him there on his horse, he will die."

"Who has shot him?"

"His name is Foster. He is the trapper who tears out the beaver dams and tears open the houses of the beaver. He is the one who digs away the side of hills in the earth, to build an easy place to store his furs. He is the one who destroys the streams and the fish, and leaves nothing for the Shoshone to hunt when he leaves."

The Indian's face was impassive, but he was silent a long moment. "I have seen the places this one has been. I know the one of whom you speak. Why did he shoot at you?"

"We hunt him. It was he who took rifles that keep shooting

to your enemy the Crow. It was he who persuaded them to come into the country of the Shoshone. He sought vengeance against the man named Stubby Rudabaugh. It is he that Washakie as given the name Red Circle Of Hair."

"I know of him."

"The woman the Crow warrior, Many Thunders, took was his daughter."

"Why did he do this thing?"

"This trapper who has shot my friend is the enemy of Red Circle Of Hair. He chased him away from where he ranches. The trapper is angry. Now he has given the Crow the rifles that keep shooting. He has caused white men and women and children to die. He has shot my friend."

"You will hunt him?"

"I will hunt him. I will find him. I will either bring him to the white man's jail, or I will kill him."

The Indian stared at him impassively for another long moment. Then he nodded his head curtly. "We will take your friend to the waters that heal."

Levi frowned. "I have heard of the waters that heal. I have not been permitted to accompany my friends, the Shoshone, there."

"Where the river of wind flows down through the deep canyon, there is a place. It is farther down than the deep canyon. There is a place there where the waters that heal come hot and bubbling from the ground. It is a place of great medicine. It is not so far from this place as the white man's town of Kaycee. It is better medicine."

"My friend will live?"

There was a heavy silence for several heartbeats. Then the Indian said, "It is a place of good medicine. Strong medicine. It is a gift of the Great Spirit, this place. That is why The Gun Of Lightning has not been there, even though he is a friend of Washakie. It does not heal all things. It is not for me to say if the healing waters will make your friend live."

Levi considered it carefully. He knew the Indian was right. No matter how Jim could be conveyed to Kaycee, the trip alone would probably kill him. He would have no less chance, perhaps a better one, in the hands of the Indians. He sighed heavily. "It will be good then."

The Indian nodded curtly again. He turned and spoke more rapidly in Shoshone to the other three. His conversation with Levi had been a garbled mix of English and Shoshone, with an occasional bit of sign language thrown in as well. As soon as Yellow Spotted Pony spoke to the other three, two of them jumped on their horses and rode to the aspen grove. They returned in minutes with two long slender poles and several short ones. With rawhide throngs they began constructing a travois.

Levi turned to Jim. "Did you hear all that?"

"I couldn't understand it all. Just parts of it. You gonna let them there Indians just walk off with me?"

He nodded, cringing at the accusation in his friend's voice. "They usually know what they're doing. If they didn't think this water that heals would do the job, they wouldn't agree to take you there. They don't feel any obligation to help most folks, the way we do. That's a Christian thing, and even the ones of 'em that's become Christian don't get that part too well. But once they agree to help, for whatever reason, it becomes a matter of honor for them to do what they offer."

"Why would they help me?"

"Because I asked them to."

"Why would they help you?"

Levi hesitated. "Well, they sorta owe me a couple. I've spent one whole year, then four or five summers with 'em. Then, too, they know Foster. They want him gotten outa the country. I 'spect they figure it's a trade. If they help me, I'll get rid of him."

"What'd you do for them?"

Levi hesitated. He didn't like to talk about such things. On the other hand, if Jim knew, it might offer him some reassurance.

He sighed and spoke reluctantly. "We was dickerin' with Washakie and some of his braves once. They'd come for some cows that Stubby gives 'em every year. They had a couple kids along. That was one of the summers I spent with them. On the way, there was a sick mountain lion that'd snuck up through the grass after one o' the kids. He thought it'd make an easy meal, and he was too sick to hunt, I 'spect. Anyway, he made a couple jumps and was about to pounce on the kid. The kid screamed. I drew and shot the cat while he was in the air. That's when they tagged the name Lightning Gun on me. Washakie made a big thing outa me savin' his son. He gave me a war bonnet with one eagle feather in it. They figure I'm their friend, which I am, I guess."

"You still got that war bonnet?"

Levi smiled fondly. "I got it. It's got a few more feathers in it now, though."

Jim abruptly changed the subject. "I'm gonna die, ain't I?"

The question caught Levi off guard. He swallowed several times. Finally he said, "I don't know. You're feverin' already, but that's normal, and that's one thing the healing water is supposed to be real good for. I still don't think you got any busted guts. I think I'd be smellin' 'em if you did. If that's the case, then I'd say you got a chance. Especially since you won't be makin' that long trip to Kaycee."

Jim nodded. "I seen some awful wounds heal up, in the war. I seen men die from some that didn't look that bad, too."

Levi could only nod mutely.

The Indians brought Jim's horse, with the travois attached to the stirrups. The horse was skittish because of the strange contraption, but not overly so.

"I guess you'd jist as well hoist me onto that, then," Jim said, trying to sound nonchalant. "I'm a mite too peaked to get there on my own."

Levi and Yellow Spotted Pony lifted Jim as gently as possible to the travois. The Indian tied him in place so he would not slide or bounce off. Jim was sweating profusely.

He grabbed Levi's hand. "In case I don't' make it, you tell

Myra I, I, aw, naw, that wouldn't be proper. Just tell her good-bye for me."

Levi gripped his hand. "You'll make it," he said.
The words sounded false and hollow in his own ears. He turned away quickly, not trusting himself to say anything further.

He turned to Yellow Spotted Pony. "I will leave my horse here. He will not go far with the hobbles on, and there is water close."

"You will go after your enemy on foot?"

He nodded. "He's on foot. He'll likely head for high country, where it's too rough for a horse anyway."

The Indian looked at him with that same expressionless gaze, then jumped on his horse. He rode off without a word, riding slowly. The others followed. The second Indian led the horse of one brave, who remained on foot. The third Indian led Jim's horse with its wounded burden. The fourth followed, lifting the ends of the two poles at the back end of the travois. In that way it made a stretcher that eliminated most of the bouncing and shaking of the wounded man. Levi assumed they would trade off, each taking a turn carrying that end of the litter. They moved surprisingly fast, making a single file line winding down the mountain. Levi watched them out of sight. He dropped to his knees and offered a fervent prayer for the life of his friend, and of thanks for the unlikeliest of friends.

He rose with a hollow feeling still gnawing at the pit of his stomach. He kindled a fire and cooked himself some breakfast. Then he checked his horse's hobbles.

Near one side of the aspen grove was a large cottonwood tree. Beneath a large branch he laid his saddle on the ground. He slung his saddle bags across it, tied his bedroll behind the cantle, and hung his bridle from the saddle horn. He replaced his boots with moccasins, then slung his boots together with a length of rawhide and hung them over the saddle. He threw a rope up over the limb of the cottonwood and hooked the loop over the saddle horn. He hoisted the saddle up to about ten feet from the ground, and tied the other end of the rope to a nearby tree. Hanging there, it was safe from the gnawing teeth of small animals on the ground, and too far down the rope for squirrels to descend.

He arranged the lumps in his pockets where he had stashed a number of items of food. He slung his canteen over his shoulder, picked up his rifle and set out.

The trail was not hard to follow. It was the eerie sense of being here before that bothered him. He had the strongest feeling of having walked this very trail. The trees were the same. The lay of the land was familiar. He knew instinctively what the lay of the land was like over the next rise. It was as if he had lived this day before.

It had felt like that the day he and Jim rescued Myra. As they had tied their horses and crept toward the huge fire, he had that same feeling of repeated actions. It was that feeling that had turned him around just as the Indian came out of the brush behind them.

Even as he had felt the Indian die on the blade of his knife, Levi had felt as if he were reliving what he had already lived once.

Now the feeling was back. Every step felt like something he

had done before. The sounds of the birds singing were the same sounds. He knew what would meet his gaze beyond the rim of the next hill, just before he could see it. When it came into view, it was exactly as he had known it would be. He tipped his hat to the back of his head and scratched his chin. He didn't like this at all. It was too spooky.

It was then he remembered. The dream! The dream he kept having, over and over, before the word had come about the Hacketts. He had already walked this trail in that frightening, recurring dream. It interspersed with dreams of the fateful attack on his family's wagon train. He was not sure which dream bothered him the most.

He tried to remember the whole dream then, but it was too elusive. He had worked too hard to push it out of his mind. He could only remember the parts he had already relived. What reached on from here was as unpredictable as tomorrow.

For the tenth time he checked the loads in his Colt, then in his carbine. He sighed heavily and took up the trail again.

Chapter Fifteen

It was back again. The tight knot in his stomach had become as familiar as a toothache. It made the hair rise along the back of his neck, as though someone were watching him from behind. It made his steps feel as though he were walking in some dream world in which he had walked before. For two weeks Levi had dogged the steps of the unwashed trapper. Four times he had avoided ambushes, as the man had doubled back and waited for a chance to kill his pursuer. Several times he had lost the trail. The trapper had total disregard for the land, but he was a woodsman. Levi thought himself as good a tracker as most Indians, but he struggled constantly to stay on this man's trail.

He was tired. He was hungry. He was reluctant to shoot any game, lest the sound of the shot give away his location. He had relied on night-time traps to catch rabbits and birds, and on his ability to catch fish quickly. There were berries as well, but they took too much time to gather in any quantity. He didn't have that kind of time. Every hour he let the trail cool made it that much more difficult to follow.

The trail had led along the western edge of the Big Horn

Mountains. It held steadily north. Sometimes it led him high onto rocky promontories and by sheer cliffs that dropped hundreds of feet. Sometimes it followed along mountain streams, leading to lower elevations where timber and grass flourished. Always it was hard to follow.

Now the feeling was back. He had almost forgotten it, until it returned. It had kept his nerves on raw edges for the first couple days he had tracked Foster. Then it disappeared. Today, half way through the morning, it came again. It started as that eerie feeling of reliving the steps, the sights, the sounds he had already experienced once before. Then the sense of danger came. It was just like that first time, at the S R Bar ranch, before any of this began. It felt like a cold wind that blew into his mind, downward with a shuddering chill over the back of his neck, settling like a canker in the pit of his stomach. It brought with it a sense of unreasoning fear. It made him irritable, but cautious.

He thought they must be in Montana Territory. If not, they were close to it. That meant they were also in Crow country. Maybe that accounted for the eerie premonition of danger. He looked around again, watching the horizon on all sides for any sign of movement. There was none.

He could see the occasional tiny marks that indicated the passage of his quarry. He was growing easier to follow. Hounded by the relentless pursuit of Hill, he had grown perceptibly more tired. As he grew more tired, he became more careless.

The first week it was all Levi could do to stay on the trail. The trapper had tried every trick in the book to shake him. He had walked in rushing streams, both upstream and down, but Levi had always found where he emerged and dogged his trail. He had tried walking beneath tall timber where there was little grass to crush. He had tried walking across barren rocky slopes where there was no grass at all. Always Levi was able to spot tiny tell-tale marks of passage to keep him in pursuit. Sometimes it was no more than a small rock, overturned to reveal a side exposed to the sun less than the surrounding stones. Always it was something his uncanny eye picked up like a word on a printed page that said, "Your prey has passed this way."

He had learned a lot about the man as he tracked him. He disliked him more and more. He demonstrated total disdain for anything except himself and his goals. He showed total disregard for life, or for pain. At night he, like Levi, set traps to silently catch animals or birds for food. But each morning Levi dismantled any traps that remained unsprung, so no animals would be killed unnecessarily.

The trapper didn't bother. Several times Levi had killed or released animals the traps that Foster had left behind had caught, after he had moved on, leaving them set. It seemed to be of no concern to him at all that something would be held there, helpless. If they were lucky, a predator would find them. If not, they would die a slow death by starvation. If the trapper's snares caught more than he could eat at a sitting, he often killed them all. He ate the choicest bits of each, and tossed the rest aside. He never released a single catch without killing it, even if he had no use for it.

That sense of impending danger haunted Levi. Especially here, along this swift stream, he was nervous anyway. The constant sound of the tumbling waters wore on his nerves. The noise made it impossible to hear anything that would offer any warning. He was totally dependent on his eyes and his instinct.

The brush and trees along the stream were thick, wherever

the rocky ground permitted them to grow. Levi made use
of all of it he could for cover. It slowed him, to stay as concealed as possible and still watch for signs of the other's
passing. If his prey were not growing more tired and careless, it would have been even more difficult.

The sense of having been here before screamed at him with
every step. Vague memories of haunting dreams nagged at
the corners of his mind.

Before him a clearing stretched for two hundred yards before
the timber and brush grew again. Something about that
clearing frightened him.

He knew he was close. The trail had grown increasingly
warm the past four days. He found the trapper's camp fire
this morning while it was still red with glowing coals. That
the man always left his fire to burn itself out added to Levi's
store of accounts to settle. The one from last night was left
so recently he could almost hear the man moving ahead of
him.

Then he started following this noisy stream where he could
hear nothing.

He studied the clearing, trying to figure out why it seemed
so threatening. He studied the edge of brush at its far side,
but saw nothing move. He fidgeted, knowing he was too
close to sit here, trembling at the ghosts of old dreams, while
the distance widened between them.

He peered from behind a tree as he studied the scene.
Unable to put substance to his fears, he sighed heavily and
stepped out. Even as he moved to step into the open, a scene
from that nagging dream flashed across his mind.

In the dream he had been in just this place. He had stepped from behind just this tree. He remembered it with a rush. In the dream, as he stepped into the open he saw a puff of gun-smoke from the plum thicket at the far side of the clearing. That was when he always started awake, sweating and trembling.

Now, as he moved to make that fateful step, the scene from the dream played itself in a flash across his mind. Instinctively he dropped sideways to the ground.

As he dropped, he saw that puff of smoke from the plum thicket. He heard an angry buzz zip past his ear. As he hit the ground the roar of a .50 caliber Sharps reached his ears. He rolled back behind the tree. He leaned his head back against it, sweating profusely. His breath came in short gasps.

The realization the dream had saved his life swelled within him. He swallowed, and felt like he was going to be sick. Bark splintered from the tree beside him. The roar of the Sharps sounded above the noise of the stream again. Levi swore and swiped at his face, where flying slivers of wood had grazed him. He made a quick lunge away from the clearing, into the denser cover of the brush, then stopped to consider his situation.

He played back the lay of the land in his mind. Like most men of his breed, he had the ability to close his eyes and see with precision and detail the land as he had last had opportunity to see it.

His assailant had chosen his ground well. The stream made an open and difficult barrier to his right. The depth and current made it impossible to cross quickly. It was too open to cross without being a perfect target, for as long as it took the hidden trapper to hit him.

At the other side was a steep canyon wall. It had been there, drawing ever closer, for the past couple miles. To circle to the left would mean either climbing that wall in full view, or circling so far back around there would be no predicting the other's position by the time the circuit was accomplished. Straight ahead was a two hundred yard wide clearing of low rocks and sparse growth. An Indian could not crawl across that open ground unobserved. It was a perfect site for the trapper. It was perfectly terrible for Levi.

As Levi thought about it, something else niggled at him. Something about that canyon wall kept skirting the corners of his mind, but he couldn't put his finger on it.

"I wonder how long he's gonna wait, and when he's gonna decide it's time to put some distance between us again," he muttered to himself.

He moved cautiously back farther into the brush. When he was sure it was safe to do so, he rose to his feet. Walking silently in spite of the stream's covering noise, he retraced his steps several hundred yards.

When he was certain he was no longer visible to his assailant's position, he moved to the canyon wall. From the shelter of the brush he studied it as far as he could see.

Almost parallel with where he crouched was something he couldn't quite remember seeing. There was a narrow fissure in the canyon wall. It contained several small clumps of brush, but little else for any foothold. Nonetheless, Levi thought it possible to climb.

The problem was, could he climb it quickly enough, quietly enough to keep Foster from figuring out what he was doing? If the trapper outguessed him, he could be waiting at the top to shoot him as he crawled helplessly over the rim. Or he could choose to run, putting a good bit of distance between them. Or he could enter the stream and backtrack. If he did that, it would take Levi as much as a whole day to find where he left the stream again.

The possibilities tumbled over each other in Levi's mind. Finally he kept low and scurried to the base of the canyon wall, opting to climb the fissure and try to circle his quarry. By the time he gained the rim of the canyon his shirt was soaked with sweat. He peered carefully over the top to be sure no one lay in wait. Satisfied, he rolled onto the grass and lay still, breathing heavily.

When his ragged breathing had slowed, he rolled onto his side. He checked the barrel of his rifle carefully to be sure no dirt had gotten into it during the climb. It was clear. He rose to a squatting position and surveyed his surroundings. The ground here fell in a gentle slope. The grass was tall and lush. Rocks poked through the grass at regular intervals. The tops of the trees along the near side of the stream showed, but from here he was completely concealed from the position of his enemy.

Nodding with satisfaction, he rose and ran at a moderate pace. When he knew he had gone well beyond the position from which his quarry had tried to shoot him, he dropped to his hands and knees. He crawled to the rim of the canyon and surveyed it from his vantage point.

He was beyond the entire clump of brush and trees in which the object of his hunt waited. He had succeeded in completely circling his position. Almost in front of him a small hogback jutted out into the canyon. It afforded a quick and easy avenue back to the canyon floor.

Looking around carefully, Levi stepped out on that narrow
ridge and followed it toward the lower elevation.Two thirds
of the way down it became too narrow to remain atop. He
squatted low to the ground and stepped off the ridge on the
side away from his opponent's position. He began to slide
almost at once. Maintaining his balance, he sat down and
slid to the bottom.

When he came to a stop at the base of the slide he quickly
checked his rifle barrel again for dirt. It didn't take much
dirt in a rifle barrel to make it throw a bullet wide of its
target. He had long since disproved the old myth that a bit
of dirt would make the barrel explode, but he knew it would
affect the accuracy of a shot.

Resisting the urge to brush the dirt from his pants, he started
walking carefully and silently toward the large copse that
held the goal of his long quest. The sense of immediate
danger was back. This time it came as reality, not some
vague premonition. It came from his certain knowledge the
hunt was nearly over. It came from the certainty that within
minutes he would have his man in captivity, or one or the
other of them would be dead.

The feeling of being lighter than air returned. His senses
were brightened. He heard and saw and smelled with
sharper acuity than anyone normally could. He felt his
blood sing as it coursed through his veins. He held his rifle
at the ready as he entered the trees. He watched all sides as
he moved stealthily forward. He knew almost exactly how
far it was to the man's position. He made no sound, even
though he knew the stream should cover any noise he made.
It took him almost fifteen tense minutes to float silently
through the dense growth. Once he had to back out of a

spot and circle around to avoid crashing through a clump of brush. He knew when he stepped around the next bush he would be in full view of his quarry's position.

"Drop the rifle!"

The voice from directly behind him doused Levi's mind with ice water. He swore under his breath and raised his arm away from his body, letting his rifle fall to the ground. He turned around slowly.

Merton Foster stood ten yards behind him. His face was haggard and as filthy as his clothes. Pieces of food and foliage were lodged in his beard. He held the Sharps rifle at his hip, pointed unflinchingly at Levi.

He laughed harshly. "I saw that crack in the canyon wall. I knowed if I missed you again, you'd shore 'nough try to circle me. I hid out over there and watched you the whole time you been sneakin' up."

Levi's mind raced. He needed to keep the man talking until he could figure out something. He just had no idea what. "Why'd you do it, Foster?"

The foul trapper laughed harshly again. "I told that two-bit rancher you'd all rue the day you run Mert Foster outa that valley. I sorta hit on the idea when I run onto Many Thunders up along the Yellowstone. I knowed he'd give his best squaw fer a repeatin' rifle, so I just offered him one. I tole 'im if'n they'd mosey down an' kill Rudabaugh's kid an' her family, I'd give a repeatin' rifle to every brave in his party. I didn't count on the rascal decidin' to keep her fer hisself, but I got even. I'da kilt you when you was slidin' down the side over there, but I just wanted you to know you ain't so hot neither."

Levi's mind had circled all the possibilities while the man
gloated. He had only one chance, and that was a slim one at
best. He knew the man was too canny to be distracted, and
too determined to be talked out of killing him or influenced.
The only chance he had was to draw and shoot before the
man could react and squeeze the trigger of the Sharps. Levi
knew he was fast. He had no idea whether he, or anyone,
could possibly be that fast.

He could see in the other's eyes he had run out of time. A
slim chance was better than certain death. He made his decision.

In a move far too fast for the eye to follow, his hand streaked
to his gun. It lifted from the holster in a smooth and fluid
motion, spouting fire as it came into line with the trapper's
chest.

The trapper took a sudden step backward. A look of confused disbelief crossed his face. Levi's .45 barked again. The
trapper fell backward heavily. The Sharps rifle fired harmlessly at the treetops as it struck the ground.

Levi stepped quickly to the man's side. He was staring in
wide-eyed stupidity at him. "How'd... you... do... do..."
He coughed. A fountain of red blood spewed from his
mouth. He made no effort to clear it from his throat. His
mouth remained open. His eyes continued their blank, wondering stare. The spark of life sputtered and quietly disappeared.

Levi emptied the spent cartridges from his pistol and
replaced them. He holstered the gun absently, staring at the
dead trapper all the while. He sighed heavily. He retrieved
his rifle and again examined the barrel for any foreign

matter. He leaned it against a tree. Grabbing the trapper's feet, he dragged him to the base of the canyon wall.

Returning to the small ridge he had descended, he laboriously climbed the canyon wall again. He went to a spot directly over the body of the trapper. Sitting down about four feet from the canyon rim, he began kicking down and away from himself into the dirt. In a matter of minutes he marked out a half-circle of ground. Continuing his assault on that marked area, he soon had a small trench separating that piece of ground from that upon which he sat. As he continued kicking, a crack appeared in the bottom of the trench. In a matter of a few more minutes, the entire segment of bank caved off the canyon rim. The body of the trapper was instantly buried beneath a couple tons of dirt and debris.

Returning to the canyon floor, he retrieved his rifle.

"Shoulda just left him for the coyotes, I 'spect," he muttered to himself. "It just didn't seem right, somehow."

He began the long trek back to where his horse waited.

§ § §

The healing was almost miraculous. In fact, Jim had healed so well he only remained with the Indians because they assured him Levi had not yet returned for his horse. When Levi rode into the encampment, Yellow Spotted Pony rode beside him.

"Why, you look finer'n frog's hair!" Levi exulted when he saw his friend. He was still gaunt, but he stood tall and strong.

"I see you found us okay," Jim responded.

"Yellow Spotted Pony was waitin' when I picked up my horse and stuff. Are you up to a ride back to the S R Bar?"

"Chompin' at the bit. Did you get 'im?"

"I got 'im."

§ § §

It was a full day later, on the road back to the S R Bar, that Jim finally approached the subject he wanted to talk about. "Uh, Levi, you bein' Myra's brother an' all… well, sorta, anyhow… do you reckon it'd be wrong fer me to… well, to set out to court her some?"

Levi smiled. "She's an awfully lonesome woman, I think. Her husband and child are dead. She's been used by that Indian, and likely figures no self-respectin' white man would want her now. She lives at home, but it really ain't her home any more. I expect she feels as out of place there as I do. She knows she doesn't have to explain anything to you, and she already trusts you. It's more than obvious that she really likes havin' you close. I think it'd be fine. In fact, if I read the signs right, I 'spect she's hopin' you will."

Jim nodded with obvious relief. He shifted his weight to ride straighter and taller in the saddle. "Are you goin' back to work for Stubby?" he asked.

Levi looked into the distance a long moment before answering. Finally he said, "Only long enough to pick up whatever pay he figures he owes me, and gather my stuff, I 'spect. I thought I might ride over to Cheyenne. That marshal's advice might be all right. Maybe I got some sort o' destiny for this lawin' thing. I thought I'd check out that Pinkerton outfit – see if maybe they need a hand."

Even as he said it, that cold wind blew the hairs on the back of his neck again. This time, though, the sensation that came with it was one of excitement and expectation, rather than warning and fear. He had found his niche in life. His destiny had met his reality.

CPSIA information can be obtained
at www.ICGtesting.com
Printed in the USA
BVHW030826200619
551526BV00001B/17/P